Who is my mother, really?

I'm staring at my mother in my tremendous defiance of her, but her eyes are fluttering round me and never look into mine. She falls silent again and throws herself back into the bed making. There is so much that she's not saying! And I'm desperate for her to speak to me!

In the still air, our unspoken thoughts are winging around us. I am aching with longing for them to come out into the open. But I'm too cowardly, or too shy, to say the first word. Too shy! Shy, with my own mother? Yes, shy, with Mammy. I look at her, Mammy who is always busy around us, flapping and swooping down on us with her words, organizing everything like she's doing now, bullying the unmade beds into neatness. Who is Mammy? I realize with a shock that I'm looking for a person *inside Mammy, a person I can talk to. And I'm too shy to say so.*

"Captures the turbulence and heartbreak of adolescence. The rich portrayals and emotional depth exhibited by her multidimensional characters make this introspective novel memorable."

—*School Library Journal*, starred review

"A passionately vivid first novel."

—*Kirkus Reviews*, pointer review

OTHER PUFFIN BOOKS YOU MAY ENJOY

Beyond Safe Boundaries   Margaret Sacks

Breaking the Fall   Michael Cadnum

Calling Home   Michael Cadnum

Celebrating the Hero   Lyll Becerra de Jenkins

Crocodile Burning   Michael Williams

The Ear, the Eye and the Arm   Nancy Farmer

Freedom Songs   Yvette Moore

Gypsyworld   Julian Thompson

A Hand Full of Stars   Rafik Schami

The Honorable Prison   Lyll Becerra de Jenkins

The Ink-Keeper's Apprentice   Allen Say

The Jazz Kid   James Lincoln Collier

Kiss the Dust   Elizabeth Laird

Let the Circle Be Unbroken   Mildred D. Taylor

The Road to Memphis   Mildred D. Taylor

Roll of Thunder, Hear My Cry   Mildred D. Taylor

Song of Be   Lesley Beake

Teacup Full of Roses   Sharon Bell Mathis

Transport 7-41-R   T. Degens

The Wild Children   Felice Holman

Won't Know Till I Get There   Walter Dean Myers

Over the Water

🪶 MAUDE CASEY

PUFFIN BOOKS

PUFFIN BOOKS

Published by the Penguin Group

Penguin Books USA Inc., 375 Hudson Street, New York, New York 10014, U.S.A.

Penguin Books Ltd, 27 Wrights Lane, London W8 5TZ, England

Penguin Books Australia Ltd, Ringwood, Victoria, Australia

Penguin Books Canada Ltd, 10 Alcorn Avenue, Toronto, Ontario, Canada M4V 3B2

Penguin Books (N.Z.) Ltd, 182-190 Wairau Road, Auckland 10, New Zealand

Penguin Books Ltd, Registered Offices: Harmondsworth, Middlesex, England

First published in the United States of America by Henry Holt and Company, 1994
Originally published in England by The Women's Press Limited, 1987
Published in Puffin Books, 1996

10 9 8 7 6 5 4 3 2

LIBRARY OF CONGRESS CATALOGING-IN-PUBLICATION DATA
Casey, Maude.
Over the water / Maude Casey.
  p. cm.
"Originally published in England in 1987 by The Women's Press Limited"
—Verso T.p.
Summary: Fourteen-year-old Mary feels like a misfit, both in England where she and
her family live and in their former Ireland home, until a visit to her Irish relatives
helps her gain a better understanding of her background, her mother, and herself.
ISBN 0-14-037589-9
[1. Mothers and daughters—Fiction. 2. Aunts—Fiction. 3. Ireland—Fiction. 4.
Farm life—Ireland—Fiction. 5. Family life—Ireland—Fiction.] I. Title.
[PZ7.C26785Ov 1996] 95-43012 CIP AC

Printed in the United States of America

*This book is for my mother and my father,
and for my daughter, Ruby Maeve.
With thanks to Peter Knight, to Gwyneth,
to everyone who looked after Ruby, to Christina,
and to all my kind and critical friends
without whom it would not have been written.
It is dedicated to the memory of Evey Scott
in her journey over the water.*

Over the Water

❧ One

We live in England, but. We live in England, but all year long we are preparing for the journey home.

When we grow out of bits of our clothing, Mammy folds them in the careful way she has and adds them to her bundles. She says, "I'll take these with us when we go home. They'll do grand for Carmel and Siobhan. They'll be delighted with them, sure."

Sometimes Mammy buys things specially, men's suits or shirts, mostly, at the church bazaars or at jumble sales, and these too she puts away into her bundles, for her brothers who work the land at home.

We snigger and we pester her:

"Mammy, why is it that they have so few things at home?"

"Mammy, don't they work hard on the land at home? Wouldn't you think they'd have money to buy their own clothes?"

"Mammy, Siobhan didn't even know what a toothbrush was when I was brushing my teeth at the well at home!"

"Whisht yer owld cod!" she says, and gives one of us a clout round the ear. I hate it when she sounds so Irish.

Carmel and Siobhan are two of our cousins at home. They are younger than us but older too, in some ways. They are expected to do a full day's work on the farm, every day, during the school holidays. And so they are used to going about on their own, and making their own decisions about things.

Whereas us lot here in England, Anne and John and me, we make no decisions about anything. Mammy and Daddy see to that.

We go to school each day and we return each afternoon. On Saturdays we go to Confession at the church, and on Sundays we go back there twice, in the morning for Mass and in the afternoon for Benediction. That is the sum total of the things we do. Daddy says, "The family that prays together, stays together." I feel as though I am drowning, drowning and suffocating.

Sometimes some of the girls at school invite me out, to go round the shops on Saturday. Mammy says, "What do you want to be doing that for, wasting your time, trailing round the streets like a shreel?" I say, "Car I go?" She says, "You can not." Sometimes one of the girls asks me to go bowling with her on Saturday night. Saturday night! I don't even bother to ask my mother. "No thanks, I'm busy Saturday night," I say, and turn away.

I'm becoming clever at lying. On Monday mornings at school, I invent outings that I've been on with my family over the weekend. I invent boyfriends and tell the girls at school of how they pop in for a coffee before Sunday lunch. I don't dare tell the truth.

Mammy knows no one in our road. She is so afraid of scornful glances at her Irish voice that she opens her mouth to no one. She says that we should do the same. "Keep your business to yourself," she says. "Don't get involved with anyone," she says. We have something to hide.

She looks over her shoulder the whole time, scanning the air for danger. She watches herself and us all the time when we're out of the house to make sure we're all doing the right thing. To make sure that we don't stand out as aliens in this foreign land.

Except for us, it's not a foreign land. We were born here, and every day we go to school.

At school, the girls are all English. They're often telling jokes about how thick the Irish are. I'm supposed to laugh. They watch me with eyes like knives, ready to strike if I show the slightest flicker of embarrassment. I want to laugh with them. I want to be one of them. But I turn my head away when I feel wild waves of anger and prickles behind my eyes.

Daddy says, "Show them you're *not* thick." So, I work late into the night on my homework, hot and heavy with exhaustion. But then they call me names if I come top in any of the tests. I have to be careful.

I'd like to talk about all this with my brother and my sister. But John is too little still, only nine, busy with his mice and his bike and his football. And Anne, well, Anne is beautiful. And if you are beautiful, it seems that you can often get away with anything. She is always surrounded by friends, with her big blue eyes and her thick blond curls that never seem to look lank or greasy. It never seems to matter when she doesn't bother to do her homework.

A lot of the time, I'm so afraid. Afraid that my lies will get found out in the end, and afraid that I'll never make friends, that I'll always be alone.

I say to Anne, "I feel as though I don't fit in anywhere." She turns her head toward me, and her eyes are so clear and blue that there's nothing in them. She hasn't got a clue what I'm on about. She's only two years younger than me, but we're so far apart.

Mammy sets us to work, Anne and John and me. We each pack a cardboard box with the clothes from her bundle. I wonder whether our cousins really will be delighted with our cast-off clothes. Myself, I hate the things that Mammy buys us, twice a year in the sales. She never lets us choose them. And when I give my opinion on what I'd like to wear, she makes me feel as though anything I might want is wrong. I have started to make a few clothes for myself this year, simple things like miniskirts. But she makes such a fuss whenever I try to get her to buy me some material.

We tie the boxes with twine and seal them with wax, ready for the journey. Our hands sting with the memory of how the string of each of these boxes will wear itself into red welts in the palms of our hands as we carry them through trains and boat in the endless hours of darkness.

I decide to wear my newest miniskirt on the journey. Such a fight I have with Mammy.

"Sure, Granny'll have a heart attack seeing the spread of you, showing the brazen legs on you up to your behind!"

"The way you go on, Mammy, you'd think it was a mortal sin for people to even *have* legs in Ireland!"

"God forgive you for your blaspheming talk! Sure what have I done wrong, to be rearing such a pigheaded strap of a girl!"

In the end, we reach a compromise. I will wear the miniskirt until we are on the boat. Then I will change into my old tweed skirt, "smart and sensible" and well below knee length. When I set foot in Ireland, I will be in disguise.

In the meantime I watch Mammy preparing to go home. Here, in her own house, the wild excitement at going home is building up into a frenzy. I wonder, for the hundredth time of wondering, why it is that she never thinks of *this* house as being her home. And why she should feel so foreign here, when she's been here for years and Ireland is so near. And I wonder, for the hundredth time of wondering, in which of them is *my* true home, and whether I'll ever find it, one fine day.

❧ Two

Humping our cardboard boxes and our suitcases through teeming pandemonium, here we are in the underground. Anne and John and me, we follow Mammy and Daddy. Through the chaos of escalators and tunnels, immense crowds of people are striding in straight lines, knocking us sideways as we struggle to keep up with our parents.

I know that it is impossible for us to lose Mammy. She is drawing us along behind her with the taut wire of her frenzy, her panic to get home. Her voice shrieks down at us from higher up the escalator. She is mad with tension that we'll miss the train and so lose, oh God, our places on the passage home.

She makes me sick, our mother does, showing us up: shouting at us, wild with nerves. Why can't she just relax? Why can't she just stand and look straight ahead like all these other people, moving silently upward?

Battling through the tube, trying to get us all to stand near her, struggling out before the doors are even properly open, wedging them with her foot as she tugs us out, she is forging up the stairs. She doesn't slow down until we have stumbled along the rubbery, gray tarmac of the platform in the soaring, main-line station. And then the filthy, exhaling train spits at us in hisses as we clamber up, exhausted, and shuffle along to our compartment.

High-pitched with nerves, Mammy organizes the suitcases up to the luggage rack, and the cardboard boxes roll around our heads and shoulders as we heave them up there too. Smug and stuffed and silent, they squat there. We rub our hands, Anne and John and me, where the twine has eaten viciously into our nerve endings.

And Daddy makes his exit. Wisely, he is leaving us. He is going farther up the train, to check on the state of affairs up there.

Hunched miserably in my corner, the rough stuff of the seat is prickling the backs of my thighs through my 30-denier American Tan stockings. The spot in the middle of my chin feels like a boiling volcano, ready to erupt through the skin. It is one of those spots that swells to a red-hot lump, excruciating if accidentally knocked, and takes ages to come to a yellow head, nice and ripe for bursting. I am fingering it carefully to see if it's ready to squeeze. It isn't.

"Mary, will you leave that spot alone. You'll spread germs all over your face." She must have eyes in the back of her head. She is working flat out, as usual. We have caught the train, but still she cannot rest. She's wiping down the window frame of the compartment and every other surface which we're likely to touch. She's brought damp cloths and Dettol, specially.

Anne is saying, "I can't get to the toilet over all those people. The corridor's packed!" Mammy's hands are flying as she pulls her back. "What's the matter with you? Haven't you a tongue in your head? Sure you're quick enough to use it when it suits you! Why can't you ask them to let you get past? Anyway, you can't use the toilet till the train is moving. Sit back down and stop your gawping."

John starts to giggle. "All the people on the platform could watch your wee splashing down on the tracks like an old horse!" He's laughing helplessly at the thought, tears squeezing out of the corners of his eyes, and writhing out of Anne's way as she elbows him viciously in the side. "I'll tell Daddy what you said!"

Mammy is lunging at John for his crudeness, waving a wet cloth wildly round his dodging head, pulling Anne off him. "Lord help me, what have I done to get such mannerless eejits for kids!"

She's back at the window now, attacking its every reachable surface with antiseptic. And John is grizzling that he can't look out of it with her in the way. He wants to see the smoke and the steam and the stricken faces looming past, hunting for a seat. He wants to hear the voices calling to each other like seabirds from platform to train, and the interesting sounds of weeping as messages are wailed from those who are about to be left behind.

Mammy's hand wrenching him down is as nippy as a pair of pliers. "John, will you sit still till I've done this, for the last time of telling you! And keep your fingers away, in the name of God! It's filthy! Filt'y! A filt'y crowded train, with nowhere in the length of it to slake your thirst with a drop o' tay in the whole long and woeful night!"

Her fierce hand is wiping along the ledges of the windowpanes, drawing the cloth firmly back and forth. Her hand curls and pinches into the corners, gripping the greasy smog into the cloth.

"But sure, it's good enough for the bloody Irish. The bloody bog Irish don't know any bether, sure." Her voice is freeing itself from being in England. "Give 'em any owld bit o' filt' an' let 'em rot in it! The dirty Irish!" I am embarrassed by this Irish voice. "Mammy, for goodness sake, don't carry on," I say.

"Carrying on, is it!" Her eyes lunge at me. "Carrying on? Sure Lord help us and save us, what kind of bloody kids have I rared at all? Ah John, will you whisht! For the last time of telling you!" and she slaps the back of his leg as he squirms to get a look out past her while she's distracted.

Miserably we slump here, Anne and John and me. Waiting to begin the journey home. I shift my bum to ease the scratching of the harsh seat on my legs. I almost wish I'd worn a longer skirt now. And I keep quiet and say nothing. Mammy is running rings round us, and

at any moment these squabbles could flare up and explode past boiling point. So I keep my mouth shut.

I look out into the corridor at the people passing by, at
the start of their journey home. How shabby they look,
shuffling along, with their overstuffed suitcases tied
round with string. I'm glad I'm not one of them, glad of
my miniskirt and my haircut, my sharp English clothes.
I'm a visitor to this train. I don't belong here.

A couple of massive, red-faced men heave into view,
suitcases hanging from their huge hands. They are
rolling, rumbustious, and drunk, roaring a song about
the exiles returning to their homes. Their loud and
merry excitement is like a breath of fresh air in our silent compartment. I find myself smiling.

One of them catches my eye as he lurches against our
door, and he flings his arm wide to bawl at me, "I'll take
you h-o-me ag-a-ain Katle-e-e-n . . ." Still smiling, I
find myself blushing.

Mammy wrenches the rubber blind down over the window. Snap! She has blocked off my view. "What are you
wasting your time looking at them eejits for?" She drags
down all the other blinds. Sealed into our silence and our
misery, we are keeping ourselves to ourselves. The compartment whispers with the faint smell of Dettol.

When the door slides open and Daddy comes in, we
know that at last the train is about to leave. We are all

glad as it draws out of the station. Left behind now are the tatters of messages, engulfed by smoke before they can be caught by the people hanging out of the windows.

Daddy is rosy with good humor. The months of planning are behind him now, and we are on our way. The atmosphere in the compartment changes. It ripples around him as he settles himself comfortably into his seat. The sharp splinters of irritability are chased away. We are warm and cozy now, and bathed in comfortable little eddies of friendly activity.

"Sit down now, Bridie," he says. "Relax! You're on your holidays! Anne, look at this map and work out where we're going. John, get your pencil and work out the speed we're going at. If we leave Euston at seven p.m. and arrive at Holyhead at one a.m. and make five stops on the way, each lasting approx. five minutes . . ."

I watch Anne snuggle up next to him. He never includes me in any of his games. In this cozy scene, I'm an outsider. Not that I'd want to do any of that anyway. Childish stuff! But my eyes are prickling as I see Anne's bright curls flutter along the sleeve of his coat.

Relax, he said to my mother. But what is she doing? Tidily, she folds her cloths and puts them away into a plastic bag. Her mouth is fidgeting. I can almost hear her thinking. The meal is being organized in her mind. The thermos, the sandwiches, the fruit, the tablecloth, the flannels. Is the little table under the window clean enough to lay the sandwiches out on? Will there be enough of the cheese sandwiches to go round? She should have nipped round to Cullens to get some more, just to be on the safe side.

I see how these countless small and repetitive tasks are wearing lines into Mammy's face, around her eyes and mouth. I can't bear it. I say, "Mammy, I'll do that," as I lean toward her. "You will not!" she snaps, and shoves me back into my seat.

My eyes are boiling with angry tears. I am drowning in frustration.

Only when she's unpacked it all does she let me help. I share out the food and the napkins. I follow her stream of criticisms and instructions. "Give those to Daddy, no, no, not those, the others. John, don't be holding your food like that! Put it in your lap, on the serviette." On and on she goes, controlling the dishing out of food.

And while we eat, her eyes swoop over us all. She is monitoring who has nearly finished, who is chewing with their mouth open, who is dropping bits on the floor, who wants salt, who should wipe their fingers with a flannel. She scolds and she chivvies. Daddy sits, oblivious.

How *can* he be so oblivious? With his legs stretched out comfortably in front of him, he puts out his hand automatically for more when he's finished what he has. He is being waited on hand and foot. He is in a good mood.

Beaming cheerfully, he is telling us a story. "Did I ever tell ye all about the time I went home to fetch your uncle Seamus back here to work with me? No? Well, here's a new one for ye, then.

"It'd taken me the whole year to save up the passage money, return fare for me, one way for him. Course, that was before I had this job on the railways. Now I can take the whole lot of you back and forth on a free pass, as you know."

Mammy darts in. "Yes, and aren't they lucky!" She is glaring at us, goading us into gratitude, but we all ignore her. "Aye, well," continues Daddy, "sure my brother Jim had never seen a train before, never mind a big boat. He was only a little fellow sure, twelve or thirteen or thereabouts, and not much bigger than you, John."

Mammy glowers at us. "Think yourselves lucky that none of *you* has to go out to work." Once more, we ignore her. We listen to Daddy.

"Sure, Jim had seen nothing in his life but the four lane ends, and the mountains beyond. So off we set anyway, and we caught the train to Dublin. In those days the journey was very long, stopping everywhere along the way, and the guard having a bit of a chat at every halt. Didn't Jim fall asleep with the length and the stretch of it, and when he woke up, wasn't the train due to run into the station in Dublin. 'Look out the window, Seamus,' says I, 'and see if you can see Dublin's fair city.'

"So, he looked and he looked until he was dizzy with all the buildings moving past. Finally he sits down and he says, 'Ah no, we're not in Dublin yet, sure.' 'Are we not?' says I, in some surprise at him. 'Are you sure now, Jim, for isn't this a fine big place we're after passing into here?' 'Ah no,' Jim repeated. 'This is a fine big place, right enough, but the name of it is "Bovril." There's a big signpost back there saying as much!' "

Daddy is shaking with laughter by the time he gets to the end of his story. Anne and John are giggling too. It's easy for us to see how Jim could have made a mistake like that. Coming from the faraway little house tucked into the skirts of the mountains in the west, he'd never heard of advertising hoardings, much less seen them.

But I'm furious. If any of the girls at school heard this story, it would confirm their worst suspicions. Even Mammy is smiling, but I refuse to laugh.

An hour or so later, we are all supposed to settle ourselves down to sleep. Mammy has a fight with the big blind at the window which looks out over the tracks. The blind wins; it refuses to stay down. So, as my family sleeps, their huddled shadowy bodies are periodically swept by staccato lights whenever the train hurtles through nameless stations. We sweep through streaming ribbons of brightness which give nothing away. Mammy and Daddy sleep deeply, despite the awkwardness of having to stay seated, with their heads lolling against the headrests. Anne and John fling out their limbs, innocent and gentle in their dreams.

I alone am awake, and grateful for my reflection in the dark window. My face is swimming, huge eyed and unmoving, against a rushing background of telegraph poles which rise and fall along the soaring, black embankments. The sound of the rails beneath my seat is pitching and tossing me into a shallow marsh of dreams.

Brown shadows are seeping in from the corners of the compartment. They advance upon me, billowing, and I am whirling in a dream of flight, shot through with shards of dread. I open my eyes, and my face is gazing at me, unmoving. It is the face of a refugee, staring unblinking into an unknown future.

When the train stops at Rugby-Midland or at Crewe-this-is-Crewe, the nasal announcements of the station staff seem to be speaking from the guard posts on a frontier. A frontier which is sinister with incomprehensible to-ings and fro-ings in the dark, wet night.

I watch as men call to each other on the dark platform outside: a hand flung up here, a head being scratched there, mail trolleys being pushed at a run along the platform. The faces of the men are tight with tiredness. They are almost like masks. And yet I know that each of these men, behind his mask, has a life, a family, rooms to call his own, cupboards whose secrets are his alone. Each of these men has his own life story gathered inside him, his likes and his dislikes, which I shall never know. And I shall never see these men again.

I could almost be watching a film of this train journey, sitting here in my seat, watching this screen, for all that I'm part of what is going on out there. Journeys like this are so strange; you see people, and their lives skim yours for an instant and then pass you by, never to be seen again. It's not a film; that can be replayed—these people are real, and their gestures are happening once and for all. It's done: they've loaded the train, see, and now the guard is raising his flag and he's blowing his whistle, and its piercing shriek is pulling us past him. We are moving along the platform, leaving him behind, and that was the past, which can never be refound.

I am shivering as I think of time and of eternity, and of how time slips away but eternity goes on and on and on, forever. Why can't I be asleep like Anne, like John? I want to shake all these splinters of fear and anxiety from my head. I want to curl up under my mother's arm, like I did when I was little. Safe, and with no worries at all. I want these two open eyes of mine to close. These two eyes which watch, which see too much.

When I was little, I had a life of my own and saw no further than that. I used to get up in the mornings and live through the days without a care. Meals came from somewhere and bedtime ended the day. My eyes accepted all that they saw.

Yet here I am now, awake, while all my family sleeps. And through this black glass, which is smeared with the rush of time, there are no safe answers. Only the cold reflection of my own loneliness.

■ ■ ■

We have turned left into Wales now; we have left England behind. The hard metal track is pulling us nearer to the searing yellow docklight of the harbor at Holyhead. Beyond Holyhead there is the water, and beyond that there is Ireland.

I am still awake, and they are all still sleeping. Above their heads, below the string hammocks where our luggage rocks and bounces, there are framed pictures. Watercolors: pleasant views of places like Stratford-on-Avon and Walton-on-the-Naze. English-sounding places, with trees and old churches and gay clouds, solid with honey-colored stone and blustery with a tang of holiday freedom.

They are cozy with the Englishness of crumpets and tea, of evening fires and Agatha Christie, of everything being all right in the end. I wish I was going somewhere like that for my holidays. To swing on a hammock under a spreading oak tree, and then order three kinds of jam *and* cream for my tea. The thought of the icy black water ahead makes me shiver.

And now, with aching shoulders and gritty eyes, we have all been disgorged from the overcrowded train. There are many hundreds of us. We are exhausted, and few of us speak. All you can hear is the steady tread of our feet on the boards of the wooden platform.

My arms are screaming from the weight of the cardboard boxes. I can barely raise my head. My feet go one in front of the other along the boards. The timber is thick and solid. But it has been worn into channels by the thousands of feet which have already passed this way.

I keep my eyes on the backs of Daddy's legs, with their wide trousers flapping in front of me. My own legs are moving of their own accord, drawn into motion by the hundreds of legs around them. John's hand is clinging to the hem of my coat behind me so as not to lose me. His awkward stumbles jerk in the back of my neck.

Suddenly, the long, deep swell of the ship's siren billows in the air around us. It is a heartrending sound, full of exile and separation, full of escape and salvation. I raise my eyes to the sky, to the dark, salt-blown void behind the glare of the harbor lights. Somewhere in that blackness, in that silent, spray-flung entrance to the wide ocean, a massive ship is looming. Its siren is telling us it's waiting. It's telling us that the passage home is near.

Exhaustion forgotten, the people around me pick up speed. I can feel the wire connecting me to Mammy. We tramp along the platform to the darkness and the ship. I keep my eyes down. In between the gaps in the timbers, I can now see the sudden black glint of water beneath my feet. We have left the land behind. We are walking over water. I can taste the salt upon my lips.

The bulk of people grows denser and moves more slowly as we are funneled into the narrow passageway leading to the gangway. John is crying in fright behind me. I put one foot in front of the other on the wooden ridges of the gangway. I am thinking, this is my first step, leading me to Ireland.

I drop one of my boxes to cling onto the rope. The rise and fall of the water against the side of the ship is pulling my stomach into my throat. I am afraid, afraid of falling into the inky blackness which is slopping beneath me.

✒ Three

Daddy and I are standing on the deck in the darkness as the boat plows through the churning sea. He is staring at the thin black line of the horizon, where Ireland will appear when the night is over. All around us there are people standing silently, shoulders hunched against the wind, their eyes hungering for a far-off glimpse of land.

Daddy turns and looks at them. His face is gray; his mouth is tight; there is no merriment in his eyes. He sighs and says, "Hunger and poverty drove us all away, Mary. And now we can only return once a year, as exiles." I shiver as I watch the water, furrowed by the prow. It swells against the towering sides of the ship and crashes down in eddies of slapping spray. I don't want to listen to him.

"We should have been able to stay there, Mary. We should have grown there, like the young hare in the green fields. But the rulers of England took it all away."

The seagulls are piercing the wind with their sharp wails of sorrow. I'm sick of all his old talk of the past, but I'm pinned down by his words. "They took our land away, and then made us till it for them, made us grow the waving corn for their own use. And all we could grow for to fill *our* bellies was the potato, on the few barren acres they left for us to use."

I can't stop my ears from his words, which lash me with the flattening wind. "And when the potato crop failed—not just once, but three years in a row—devastated by a terrible disease called the blight, what could we do then, Mary? Tell me, what could we do?"

He's talking of things that happened a hundred years ago, talking of them as though they happened to him! His hand is clenched, beating upon the rail as he thumps the words home to me. "Three years in a row, the potato crop rotted in its stinking pits! And the people watched the fields they'd tilled grow ripe and full and golden with corn. And they saw fleet after fleet of ships leave Ireland, bursting with the rich grain, the oats and barley from the fields of Ireland. Taken to feed the coffers of the English, while them that had grown it grew hollow eyed with hunger."

My stomach is churning with irritability at him as the deck throbs beneath my feet. I want to go back below decks to the cozy cabins, with Mammy and John and Anne. But his voice is relentless. "Famine stalked the land then, Mary, and the people grew too weak to work to pay the rent for their patches of land. And the agents of the landlords came and evicted them, tore down the roofs of their homes, scattered the ashes from their hearths and cast out their few bits of furniture and their cooking pots, off out into the mud."

He's shaking his head, as full of grief as if it was all his own story. "Sure God in heaven, the hearts must have died in the people then, cast off their land, huddling in the ditches at the sides of the roads, little children too, with nothing but the poor rags they stood up in. And in these unsanitary conditions, the fearful specter of disease soon took hold of them."

The wind is plucking at my head and mouth. "Thousands of living skeletons were roaming the land, Mary, trailing the shroud of disease behind them. And what did the English rulers do? Did they open the bursting sacks of grain and give food to the starving? Did they tend to the sick and the dying? Did they?" His hand clutching my arm is like a vise. I shake him away from me.

"Daddy, stop, you're hurting me!" I shout at him. "Stop going on like this! I *know*! I know it all! There's no need for you to keep on at me!" But Daddy's face is probing mine like the sharp beak of a seabird, though he loosens his grip on my arm. "Mary, I'm telling you this so that you'll never forget how it was that your people first had to leave their land. Did the English rulers help those starving people? No, they did not! What they did was to commission ships and herd the people onto them, the sick and the dying, packing them into the stinking holds without enough food or water to last the journey. And they sent them away, away from Ireland, across the Atlantic Ocean."

He takes his hand away from me and scans the swelling seas around us. "Aye, they were the first to be torn from our land. And they died in thousands on that voyage to hell, in the stench of disease, and their grave was the icy water of the North Atlantic." He turns to me again. "And if I'm telling you this, it's because those dead souls have no monument to their suffering save what we carry in our own hearts, Mary, all of us, now. And because those of us who have survived to this day still have to leave Ireland in shiploads. Driven out by poverty, the hearts in us dying till we can set foot on our land again. Because still, to this day, our land is not free."

He is silent then, and I cannot move until at last he turns to go back down to the cabins. My teeth are chattering, and there are ghosts hovering and keening in the wind above the water, darting in and out of the spray over the Irish Sea.

&Four

I am glad that the night is over. These past few hours
fear has been throbbing in the wake of the boat like a
stain of dark woad, seeping in from the past and engulf-
ing the future.

But now, at last, the dawn has come. Its gentle violet
wash has lightened the sky, and the trailing clouds are
tipped with pink. Everything is suspended; we are so relieved. We are all holding our breath, leaning over the
rails of the deck in this timeless moment which seems to
have the power to turn wishes into magic.

And now, quite suddenly, the sea is dazzling and
glinting with light. The swell is patterned with glinting
honeycombs of gold. All around me people are yearning
for their first glimpse of Ireland. And now, quietly, the
mountains of Dublin are moving forward through this
lambent light, and Ireland is drawing us to her, across
the water.

Mammy issues her stream of criticisms and instructions,
and somehow we disembark. We shuffle through the
customs shed and onto the little train that takes us from

the port to the city center. From here, we have to go to another station in a taxi to catch our last train. The one that will take us from Dublin to the end of our journey, in County Kilkenny. Our parents are racing to the taxi rank.

"Misther! Misther! Carry yer bags! Misther! Carry yer bags!" Little boys are swarming round us. Their shrill cries fly up like birds into the vaulted roof of the station, swooping past the statue to the heroes of the Rising, who almost, but not quite, won freedom for the whole of Ireland fifty years ago. We are running again, after Mammy and Daddy, running the last lap home.

The little boys have bare feet, and their legs are blue and mottled, and their heads are shaved all over, not just at the back like John's. This is the capital city of our country, and these boys have nothing but their fathers' old trousers to wear, tied up around their chests with string under their armpits. They are so small I cannot imagine them carrying our heavy luggage. Their faces are sharp little blades of need. Even John is silenced, for a wonder, by their cries.

We are rushing along the platform in a chaos of steam from the vast engines. They sigh and exhale, and settle themselves into their buffers. We flee past the legs of horses waiting patiently, harnessed to their cabs on the brown, gleaming flagstones. My eyes are full of grit from the short night of sleep and the ship has given me sea legs. The ground is pitching and swelling like pneumatic rubber. I am dizzy with the rush of it.

When we reach the towering granite pillars which lead out into the road, I am halted by a row of women who stand silently there, at the entrance to the station. They are dressed in long skirts of thick, dark material and in shawls as big as blankets, which cover their heads and shoulders. The shawls are wrapped round in the front to form slings, from which peep the round-eyed faces of their babies. At their feet are half a dozen toddlers, playing on the ground or pulling themselves upright by their mothers' skirts.

The women stand perfectly still, like carvings. Their feet are bare, and each one has a hand held out in front of her. Silently they stand there, in the passive pose of beggars. But there is no demand for pity coming from them. In fact, there is something in the dignity of the way they are standing, and in the full folds of their plaid shawls, that fills me with respect. They are asking for what should be theirs by right—food and shelter for their children—not charity or pity. In the palms of their hands they are holding the history of all the people who have ever lost their freedom.

Suddenly I realize that I have been standing there stupidly, gawping at them with no manners. I feel myself blush with shame as one of them turns her head toward me. Black hair frames a white forehead, under which the eyes are astonishingly blue. I stand there, captivated, blushing, and I hear Daddy calling me from over by the taxi rank. Awkward and stammering, I find myself speaking to the woman. "We're over from England. We're going home for the holidays."

She seems to find this amusing as she looks me over. "Ah well, good luck to ye, so," she says. Here in Ireland people don't say "good-bye," they say "good luck."

The journey is over now. At this little gray station in County Kilkenny. The signs are all in Irish, and the air is still and silent. "Good luck to ye," says the ticket man, and then we are out into the yard. Mammy's sister Nuala is running toward us at full tilt, high heels for the holiday wobbling around Mammy. "Jaysus, Bridie, I'm killed waiting for ye," she says, and Mammy is blushing in the wild shrieks of her sister's hug.

Her brother Billy strides forward in his tight holiday suit, arm held out to Daddy, shaking hands. "You're welcome, Liam. Good man yourself." His face is red and wide, and split in two by his smile. Her brother Joe holds back, shy, by the pony, Dadda's gray mare, holding the reins as her head tosses up and down. He is a grown man, my uncle Joe, but he is shy, and he blushes as he smiles at me.

"And here are the wasters! Sure will you look at the size of them!" Anne and John and I, we shuffle, awkward but pleased as we're turned and patted and tweaked by Nuala's fingers. "And Mary in the stockings! Sure Jaysus who'd credit it!" She can't believe how I've grown up in the year since I was last here. I'm not a child anymore.

Up into the trap we go, free at last of our burden of luggage, and we sink back against the soft leather while Billy and Joe heft and stash and lash on our suitcases and boxes with ropes.

Nuala and Mammy sit, eyes locked to eyes, hands gripped in hands across the seats. "How's Mammy?" asks my mother. She means my granny. "Ah well," says Nuala, "sure, she's grand, but her poor heart is sore." Nuala's eyes glitter, and Mammy's do too. We are sitting in Dadda's trap, being pulled by Dadda's gray mare, but Dadda has died in the year since I was last here. It is odd, not having him here with us now.

Nuala's voice is liquid, rising and falling, bubbling with news and with praise for us all. "Aren't ye grand, to have come all that way. Sure you must be murthered with the journey!" But now there is no more filth of cars or trains or throbbing engines. The chaos is over.

There is no tarmac here, just lanes of earth, and flowers brushing past the bowling wheels. And no sound save for birdsong, thrown up by the pony's hooves. The gray mare. Dadda's favorite horse. Mammy wipes her eyes and nudges me. "Will you open your mouth and fill your lungs with this air! Anne! John! All of you!" And we do.

✑ Five

So. Today is the first morning in the place that both my parents call "home." In other words, the house which belonged to Dadda, my mother's father. While we were coming here, on that long and tiring journey, it felt as though it was the first time I'd ever come. And yet it's only been a year since I was here last.

But that year has been a long one, a whole year of isolation for me in England. And I feel so different now from how I felt when we were here before. Almost like a different person. Things have changed here too since we were last here. Dadda is dead.

Mammy came back for his funeral on her own, and she told us how his body had been carried from the house all the way to the church, through the long and winding lanes, by his six sons. Three of these sons had traveled from as far away as Australia and Canada, and his daughter Shelagh came from Australia, and Nuala from New York. Mammy said at the time how sad it was that his long-lost children had returned home only to bury him. But she also said he would have been so glad to think of them all walking together down the lanes once more.

Dadda is dead, but he's only just died, really, and I can't get used to the idea of him not being here. Neither can Granny, it seems. She was crying when we arrived here yesterday, and she said to me, "Mary, poor Michael is gone." Michael was his name. I didn't know what to say. I can't imagine him not being here, off out working in the yard somewhere, with his voice reaching me through the open window. It was so strange yesterday not being met by him at the station, and his gray mare bringing us here as though nothing had happened.

Dadda built this house, and when I say "built" I don't mean that he paid someone else to do it. He did nearly every job himself, with his own hands. He cut the stones it's made from, and he harnessed an ass to the grindstone down the lane to grind every bit of the mortar which binds the stones together. He made the window frames and the doors, and he cut the long planks that make the floors and the ceilings. So it's no wonder, really, that I can still feel him all around me.

In this room, the big bedroom upstairs, he made the ceiling so beautifully, in a pattern. Slim planks go round the four sides of it to make a border, and from the four corners of this border Dadda slanted more planks into the center, sloping them so that they radiate from the big hook in the middle, where the brass lamp hangs.

Lying here in bed, my gaze wanders over Dadda's

ceiling. This big bedroom is where my whole family sleeps, in three beds for the five of us, when we are here. But at the moment I'm alone, and this is most unusual, because in my family we are never allowed to have lie-ins, usually. So what a treat it is for me to be alone in this bed, able to stretch out my legs until the muscles smile, without kicking my sister in the face. When we're here, Anne and I have to sleep top to toe in the one bed. This is all right so long as we're not fighting. But it's even better to be able to stretch out my limbs into the four corners of the big bed, and to feel the cool sheets skimming my skin. I feel as strong and supple as a cat, and my skin feels as clear and smooth as spring water.

I'm here because my period started in the night. I still can't work out when they're due exactly, but I wasn't surprised when I felt it start after that hot and throbbing journey. I had to wake Mammy up after getting out of bed with my knees squeezed together to stop the blood getting onto Granny's sheets. Mammy was flummoxed, but luckily she had some STs, so I put one inside my knickers and got back into bed.

When I woke up this morning, she seemed embarrassed. She hustled and bustled until she'd got Daddy and John out of the room, and then she said to me, "You stay in bed there, Mary, and I'll bring you up a drop o' tay." Anne, of course, was furious, "Why is she allowed to stay in bed and not me?" "Whisht," said Mammy. "She's got the bellyache."

And indeed that's not far from the truth, either. I do feel as though all the energy in my body has dropped down into my belly. Great dragging pains are pulling at me there, and tugging at my thighs. But my head feels quite light, as though a great weight which I've been carrying has lifted from my back, and as though a tight band has loosened itself from around my forehead.

So I'm glad I'm allowed to be alone up here, in this sun-dance morning which is cool and flickering with light. I don't really know why Mammy has let me stay in bed; perhaps she's embarrassed in front of Daddy and John. But I'm loving it here. The window opposite my bed fills the space from floor to ceiling, and light is streaming in, sieved by the lace of the curtains to make golden patterns on the wooden floor and the white-washed walls. A soft breeze is wafting in, belling the curtains, which undulate gently, like waves, and its gentle trail across my face makes my heart ripple.

I feel so peaceful; alone, yes, but not lonely, in this room. Everything around me is a pleasure to look at. As I let my gaze stretch down over my bed, over the hills and valleys of my counterpane, it feels as though I am looking down over a continent. A whole continent over which I can pass the palm of my hand, and reach for anything I want.

Granny made this counterpane, and the thick lace curtains, and the embroidered cloths on the chest of drawers, and the little rag rugs which dapple the floor. Mammy often says, "It beats me how she did it, with nine kids to rear, and the farm to run, and all the cooking and the cleaning and the washing to be done, all by hand, with no gas or electric or running water." And now I think about it, I am also wondering how she managed it, because she's still hard at it, still hauling every drop of water from the well by herself, though she's seventy years old.

But lying here in bed, it does seem as though anything is possible. Leaning back against my pillows and drinking my tea, I feel as luxurious as a film star, tra-la! After all the misery of the journey over, it seems to me a miracle that I should now be feeling such quiet peace. Perhaps the woman at the station in Dublin yesterday has something to do with it. There is such a gentle feeling of excitement in me, like the singing waters of a brook that bubbles gaily over stones.

Perhaps my period has something to do with it. I feel so rich with possibilities, as though I could do anything, as though I'm on the verge of a great adventure. I feel so proud of myself, as though I'm growing up at last. No wonder I feel different. After all, when you're grown up you can do anything you want, without anyone bothering you. Anything in the whole world!

✄ Six

My pleasant reverie has been cut short! The door clatters open and in bustles Mammy. She's carrying the small tin bath and a bucket of hot water. I smile at her. How kind she is, bringing me hot water here upstairs so that I can wash in peace!

But she is carefully avoiding my smile as she walks across the room to the fireplace without looking at me. She puts the bath and bucket down upon the hearthrug, although there is no fire laid up in the grate, and she takes a towel from out of the press. She says, "Get out of bed now, and come over here."

I slip out of bed, though I'm sorry to leave it. As I go over to her I see that she has a rosary beads in her hand, and that she's pulling another one from her pocket. Questions leap into my eyes, but she's avoiding them.

"Kneel down here," she's saying, "and we will say the rosary, to Our Lady." She looks up and I follow her gaze to the statue of the Blessed Virgin on the mantelpiece. It's one of those luminous ones that glow in the dark. She kneels down, but I'm still standing, dangling the beads in my hand, bewildered. She yanks at my night-dress; her voice is harsh. "Will you kneel down here, Mary, when I'm telling you! Get down on your knees and pray to the Blessed Virgin for purity!"

What does she mean? "For purity"? I look down at her. "What do you mean, Mammy?" I ask. She ignores me completely and yanks me down, so hard that I almost fall on top of her. There is so much that she is not saying as she bends her head and begins in on the prayers. What does she mean?

Wild surges of anger and resentment are beating at my brain as I kneel there beside her on my bare knees. But she's off at full tilt on the prayers; there is no point now in arguing with her. So I mumble and sigh with her through the whole bloody rosary. When we get through all five decades to the final "Glory be to the Father," etc., I breathe a sigh of relief and start to get up, but she yanks me down again and we're off on the Litany of Loretto.

I can't bear it. I am so angry with her, so bored at the droning prayers, so mad at her power over me. I am almost choking. She is looking at me as she says the words, waiting for me to repeat them after her. But each time I try to challenge her with my eyes, she jerks her head up to look at the statue, her mouth rigid as she waits. It seems that I have no choice.

I get the words out eventually. I manage the first part all right, but when she gets to the bits about "Mother most pure, Mother inviolate, Mother most chaste," I find that I cannot say them. My throat has just closed up completely.

I am tortured with conflict. Sweat breaks out on my forehead. There she is, looking daggers at me, barking "Virgin most prudent" between her clenched teeth. But I know that she won't actually interrupt the prayer to say anything to me. And I cannot bring myself to say the words after her. I want her to stop. I want her to stop and ask me *why* I can't say these words. I want her to have a conversation with me.

But she is carrying on with the prayer alone. The dilemma is making my head swim, and my face is getting redder and redder. I know that I'm upsetting her, but I also know that if I say those words, it will feel like lying. And something in myself will be betrayed.

So on she goes, alone, until I hear her say the bit about "Mystical rose," etc. I swallow then. I've always thought that those particular lines are more like poetry than anything. They don't feel like chains to bind you down, like all the others do. So I start to whisper them after her, and somehow we get to the end.

I don't dare to look at her as I wait for the bombshell to drop. "What in God's Holy Name is the matter with you?" she hisses at me. "Have I raised a brazen child that won't even say her prayers to God's Holy Mother?"

"But Mammy," I reply, trying to stop my voice from trembling, "you haven't said *why* I have to say these prayers today. We never usually do, and no one else has said them this morning."

"Quit acting the eejit," she snaps, shoving her beads back into her pocket. "You know full well why so!"

But I don't. Oh yes, I know that it must have something to do with my period from the way she is avoiding my eyes, but she never made me do this when my period first started, in England. Then, she gave me a book with Our Lady on the cover and muttered darkly about letting boys touch me, and about how I had to hide my STs from Anne and John, but she's never made me say the rosary with her like this before.

I want to shout at her, "No, I *don't* know!" I want her to explain to me exactly what she means. But I am too cowardly. I glare at the statue and wrestle with myself. I am surprised that Mammy hasn't carried on shouting at me, like she usually does when I've disobeyed her, getting me by the scruff of the neck and shaking me. Instead, she is flinging blankets off the beds and shaking pillows. She has distanced herself from me.

And I am too cowardly to bring her nearer again by challenging her with a direct question. But I won't let go of my resentment at the prayer. The mild gaze of the statue is annoying me too much for that. So I say, "Well, anyway, why do all those prayers keep going on about mothers being pure, and chaste and so on? And the mother of God being a virgin! Doesn't God think that normal mothers are good enough, then?"

She stands up abruptly and says, "God help us, but you're a terrible precocious strap of a girl, so y'are, to be questioning the will of God Himself." I'm staring at her in my tremulous defiance of her, but her eyes are fluttering round me and never look into mine. She falls silent again and throws herself back into the bed making. There is so much that she's not saying! And I'm desperate for her to speak to me!

In the still air, our unspoken thoughts are winging around us. I am aching with longing for them to come out into the open. But I'm too cowardly, or too shy, to say the first word. Too shy! Shy, with my own mother? Yes, shy, with Mammy. I look at her, Mammy who is always busy around us, flapping and swooping down on us with her words, organizing everything like she's doing now, bullying the unmade beds into neatness. Who is Mammy? I realize with a shock that I'm looking for a *person* inside Mammy, a person I can talk to. And I'm too shy to say so.

She straightens up now and walks over to the bed I share with Anne, saying, "Anyway, don't be bothering your head with such things. Just make sure that you get down on your knees every day while you've got this thing and pray to Our Lady for purity."

"This thing!" Is that all that she has to say, while I'm here longing for her to talk to me? She's pulling herself even farther away from me. I hear her say: "And don't be lounging about in bed, either. Sure, God can see deep into the recesses of your heart and mind—even when you've the bedclothes pulled up over your head."

Does she really think I can still be frightened by stuff like that? She used to give me nightmares when I was small, saying that to me as she went out the door after tucking me up in bed. But not now! Now she is insulting me, with her talk to frighten children. But she has given me a way of getting back at her. I want to hurt her, since she won't let me near her.

So, trembling with boldness, I laugh and say, "Ha! What does he want to be looking under there for, under my sheets? Hasn't he anything better to do with his time?"

Now I *have* gone too far. She lunges at me, really wanting to throttle me, shouting at me. "God help us, what have I done wrong to raise you to such wickedness, and the Holy Virgin Herself sitting up there listening to your shameful words! Come here till I get you! I'll put manners on you if it kills me!"

I dodge her around the bedroom, saying, "Mammy, ah no, don't, I'm sorry, leave me alone!" The tears are close to falling, and who knows how it would have ended, when suddenly, salvation! There is an uproar from the yard outside.

Mammy pauses, her face flushed, her hand still lunging toward me, but her ears are at the window. Men's voices are raised, and there is the sound of horses' feet scraping the concrete of the yard. "Get back! Back wit' ye!" My uncle Billy's voice comes up to us, and Mammy turns and flies to the window.

"Begod, aren't they after bringing in the stallion from the meadow," she says, "and he the powerful demon." She pulls down the sash window and leans out, calling to her brothers who can't hear her, adding her contribution to the general mayhem. I stand beside her and see my three uncles guiding the stallion through the yard to the well house. Uncle Pat-Joe, the father of Siobhan, Orla, and Carmel, has come here from his own house to help with it, it seems. He and Billy are at the head of the stallion, drawing at ropes attached to the halter on either side. Uncle Joe is at the rear, nimbly edging the stallion sideways with the help of a long, slim switch.

"Ah Bill!" shrills Mammy, "will you mind his back legs, for the love of God! His ears! Lookit his ears, lying flat! Ah, will you mind! Begod, isn't he mad for the mare!"

Dadda's mare is whinnying from across the wall, where she must be tethered to the creamery cart, and the stallion hauls up his head from the wrenching ropes and lets rip with a scream in reply. "Surely Jaysus, isn't he a fierce powerful beast," says my mother. "God love him," she adds. I look at her, hanging out of the window with her eyes bright with excitement, and for a second I think she is like a young girl, and not like Mammy at all.

The stallion is mad at being confined in the mesh of ropes at his head, but his rage is doubled when my uncles get him inside the well house and shut the door on him. They fasten it securely, and then they wedge a spliced pine trunk full across the width of it. I feel sorry for him, trapped in there in the dark, barricaded in.

"What have they put him in there for?" I ask Mammy as she pulls up the window. We can hear the rising crescendo of his screams. "Sure, isn't it the season for the mares!" she replies with satisfaction. "He'll have plenty of customers for the next few days, of that you may be sure." My quarrel with her seems to be forgotten. She is desperate to get back downstairs, to join the men outside, to be part of the general talk that is going on by the yard gate. "Make sure you're down soon—and clear up this mess," she says, and she is off out the door.

So she has left me, and I stand here listening to the stallion shrieking. Then there is a crash: the sound of his hooves backfiring into the well house door! I look out and see that the wood of the door, heavy though it is, is trembling as his hooves blast into it with a salvo of blows. The mare is still whickering, and the sound of her voice seems to set him off worse. I see Mammy fly out of the house door, beneath my window, and she rushes off round the yard to join her brothers.

I feel exhausted, and the day has barely begun. And to think I'd been feeling so pleasant before Mammy came in! She's like a tornado that whirls around me, shakes me inside out, and then dumps me, to land wherever I fall. I'd been feeling so pleased, so almost grown up, and now I feel like crying. I feel almost dizzy with light-headedness. She can talk quite freely of the stallion and the mares and all that stuff, but she won't talk to me, except in the same code of orders and reprimands that she's used with us all since we were children.

But that stallion saved me. And now the door is still shuddering from the lashing of his hooves. I can feel it thudding in my head. I feel as though I'm drowning, I'm so confused. And as I walk back from the window the Blessed Virgin is still up there, looking at me, with her bland eyes that follow me wherever I move around the room.

✍ Seven

I pull myself together eventually and wash myself in the little bath. The water in the bucket has cooled down, and I shiver as its droplets trickle down my back. I get it over with hurriedly and rush cowering into my clothes. Jeans and a jumper for my first day on the farm.

I start at the knock on the door. In my family no one ever knocks; they just come barging in. "Who is it?" I ask, and a merry voice answers me. "It's Nuala. Can I come in?" Awkwardness makes my voice sound prim as I say, "Yes, come in."

The door opens and her smile fills the room. "Well, good morning, Mary," she laughs, "and how is it with you?" I've been so locked in my wretchedness over Mammy that Nuala's greeting is too much for me. "I'm all right," I say grumpily, and turn away. She comes over to me and says, "Are you sure, now?" Her eyes are reaching for me, but she's a stranger, and I'm afraid that Mammy might have told her about my period. What business is it of hers! I keep my eyes away from her and say, "I'm perfectly all right, thank you."

Nuala is walking over to the bath. She has a lovely

face, I realize, and her thick, dark hair is in a ponytail. She looks very young, too young to be Mammy's sister. "Well," she's saying, "I heard ye lepping and roaring up here just now, yourself and your mammy, and I wondered to meself, could you do with a bit of a hand?"

She's looking at me levelly. She has freckles on the bridge of her nose. I'm astonished at her words. Is she offering me the hand of friendship? Ha, well, I won't be caught out by assuming that she is. I feel too cold inside. So I say, "Well, you could give me a hand taking the bath downstairs." She smiles at me and shrugs, and we empty the dirty water back into the bucket and then shuffle out of the bedroom, her with the bath, me with the bucket. And all the while I feel embarrassed, and even more confused.

As we go down the stairs I see that she has a bounce in her step, even though she has to negotiate the bath over the banisters. She does it airily, without making a big thing of it. I feel so sorry now that I didn't smile back at her. But I hardly know her. She's been in New York for a long time, working as a nurse. At one time we heard that she was going to marry a policeman there, but then she changed her mind. She came home for Dadda's funeral and just decided to stay, to keep Granny company in the house.

As I watch her ponytail bounce up and down, I wonder why I was so rude to her. And as she turns at the bottom of the stairs to grin at me again, I'm so glad! I'm suddenly very glad she's here.

✒ Eight

I'm sitting at the kitchen table. Outside, the men are loading the churns onto the cart to take them to the creamery. Everyone is outside, helping with the early morning work. We don't have breakfast here until all the milking has been done and all the animals have been fed. They come first. Normally I'm out there too, helping, but this morning has been different.

It's funny how easily I have slipped back into being here. I know every whorl and scratch mark on this table, and I know what is in every drawer and behind each door of the press. I know that if I slip my hand down beside the cushion of the armchair, I will find yesterday's paper there. But I also know that Dadda won't sit down there after breakfast and reach for it. He has gone, but the chair and the paper go on being here. This makes me feel very odd.

Just beside me here, attached to the leg of the table by a nail, there is a long leather strap dangling down. It is here that Dadda used to sit every morning and sharpen his razor blade along it, before shaving in front of a mirror which he'd prop up on the table. The leather strap is still here, but his wicked slim blade will never whip up and down it anymore. I'm trying to keep my eyes from glimpsing it.

Instead, I carefully look around the kitchen. It is a large and simple room, with two windows which face each other on either side. These windows have the lovely, creamy lace curtains that my granny made, hanging in front of stone sills so deep that you can sit in them. The floor is concrete, and on it stands this big table, with the forms around it, the chairs, a couple of presses—one with the wireless on top of it—and Dadda's armchair.

The walls are whitewashed, and on one of them is a picture of the Sacred Heart, with the Pope's blessing on the house written under it. Above the wireless, there is an icon of Our Lady holding the Infant Jesus in a heavy gold frame. This has a little red lamp attached to it, which Granny keeps burning day and night. These are the only pictures in the house, apart from photographs of my exiled uncles and Aunty Shelagh, which are all on the heavy sideboards in the lower room. The lower room is the best room in the house, where no one goes, except on Sundays or funerals or when the priest comes visiting.

Here there is no furniture bought for the house, unless it is essential, and no ornaments or pictures or things like that. Everything is kept to a minimum, and anything that is bought is bought only for the farm, and for the animals outside. If any of the girls in my class at school saw this plain room, I'd be ashamed of how primitive it looks.

But sitting here in it now on my own, with no one else's eyes to judge it by, I feel warm and settled. This kitchen is the center of the house. When I was a little girl, I always used to think that the center of the kitchen was called the "heart." In Ireland, people sometimes pronounce the *th* at the ends of words as *t*, so when I was little the "hearth" was the rich, warm "heart" of the house.

It takes up an entire wall, like an altar at church, only much nicer. On those cold, neutral afternoons when nothing much is happening and when the sky seems to be pressing down upon the land squeezing all the life out of it, you can climb into the hearth. You can curl up in there and dream over the fire. It has an artery too, just like a heart does: the chimney soars up from it, like the inside of a tower, and when you're inside the hearth you can look straight up and see the sky.

Granny is in charge of the heart of the house. It is she who ministers to the complicated machinery suspended over the fire. That's why I'm just sitting here, waiting for her to come in. I wouldn't dream of touching anything until she's here.

All the cooling and the heating of water and the boiling of dirty clothes takes place thanks to this machinery over the fire. And thanks to my granny's wizardry with it. The three-legged pots of various sizes hang by their handles from chains, and these chains are attached to a hoist whose hinged arm is bolted into the inside of the chimney. In the evenings, Granny mixes up mash for the young animals and for the poultry, and she mixes up porridge for us and leaves the lot to cook overnight over the slow fire.

And now the door is opening, and in she comes. She's fed the chickens and the ducks, the calves and the pigs, and she's carrying a big jug of milk, fresh from the milking. She's taking the lid off the porridge and adding some milk to it, stirring it around. I get up and greet her.

"You're welcome, allanah, and isn't it a grand day, thanks be to God, for your first morning home!" She's waving a poker at the window to salute the day properly. Then she bends down, and I watch as she uses the poker like a magician's wand between the bars of the grate, teasing little currents of air in among the embers so that the flames lick and flutter up greedily. Next, she takes some slabs of turf from the back of the fire to feed it. Air and earth she's giving, to feed the fire.

She is concentrating, and she doesn't speak, and neither do I. The scent of turf smoke is filling the room. Its delicate tendrils coil into my face and hair, and as I breathe them into me, I feel as though I've never been away. Certain smells can make you travel in time and space; as you breathe them in they seem to fill you up, like food. That's what turf smoke is like for me.

Still concentrating, Granny stands up and places her hand against the door of the bread oven which is built into the chimney breast, to test it for warmth. As I watch her, it seems to me that the sense of the fire and its rhythms is actually pulsing through her body; that it's as much a part of her as the throb in her own wrist and the beating of her own heart in her breast. She's just a little woman with gray hair, but to me she seems supremely powerful. She has her finger on the pulse of mysteries.

She breaks the spell in her own time, when she is ready. "Now Mary," she says briskly, "the whole lot of them is gone to the creamery, or up with your daddy at Pat-Joe's place up the lane. So help you me with the cake before they get back." "Cake" is the name of the bread that she bakes every morning, sometimes with sultanas in it, for eating after the porridge and the eggs and bacon. I follow her through the door into the back kitchen, exactly as if I've never been away, glad to be put to work by her, and sharing her movements as I have done a thousand times before.

The back kitchen is a cool, dark place where the food is kept, and where the washing up is done, and where all the crockery lies ranged on wooden shelves against the whitewashed wall. Granny takes a big knife from the little shelf put there specially for it, high up on the wall out of harm's way, and she begins to slice rashers from the carcase of a pig which hangs from the ceiling on a hook. I have my own little job to do and I know it well, as I stoop under the gently revolving pig and carefully scoop a metal bowl into the sack of flour on the floor.

The white cloth of the sack is printed with a large picture of a woman. She is wearing flowing robes, and she is standing, with her arms outstretched, before a blazing yellow sun whose rays burst up the bag around her. Above her in large letters is the word *Sunlight*, and below her, in smaller letters, *Patent Household Flour*. The cloth is cotton of the finest weave, to hold the flour, which swells heavily inside it. I know this cloth and this woman intimately, for it's from these flour sacks that Granny makes sheets for our beds, sewing them together when she has enough of them, so that our beds are blessed by her outstretched arms, reproduced in rows.

As I kneel in front of the sack and greet her, I think to myself that she has far more life in her than the statue of the Virgin Mary upstairs, luminous or not.

I walk back into the kitchen and put the flour bowl on the table. Then I return to the back kitchen to fetch some eggs for the breakfast rashers. Uncle Billy likes a duck egg, and these are pale and smooth as marble, greeny-blue and translucent, twice the size of the hens' eggs next to them. I choose six of these and a small pullet's egg for my brother, scraping the straw and bits of droppings from them with my thumbs. I put them all on the kitchen table in a bowl, and then get on with laying the table with the heavy cutlery and the crockery of many different patterns.

I feel quite at home as I settle down to watch Granny make the bread. Her presence is so strong and solid and the routine of these small daily chores is comforting to me. She does everything calmly and perfectly, from years of practice, and bowls and cutlery settle down peacefully under her touch, never flying onto the floor or rattling out of place, like they do sometimes when I touch them. Her hands move quietly, measuring and sorting, and her utensils stand sturdily where she has placed them. I too feel calm and useful now, and not the wild disordered thing I was earlier upstairs, with Mammy.

She mixes the flour with the soda, and then the sultanas are bobbing about under her hands as she folds them in, coating each one with its disguise of flour. The flour is so fine that it is like liquid through which her hands are floating. I watch her hands, pale and freckled, and I fiddle with the leather strap hanging from the table, feeling its smooth supple length passing through my fingers in a comforting way.

But then, with a lurch of my heart, I remember Dadda, and I drop the strap hurriedly, glancing at her sideways to see has she noticed. I feel panic tremble in my stomach, because her mouth is quivering, and she says, "Your poor dadda is gone, Mary, God bless him. May he rest in peace."

She doesn't pause in her work, though. She makes a well in the center of the flour with a little scoop of the side of her hand. Then she takes the blue jug and pours the sour milk from it into the well in a thick and lumpy stream. "Poor, poor Michael," she continues. "There was none like him, sure. Am I not vexed to know how will I manage without him at all."

I feel anxious and ill at ease because she is showing her grief to me so plainly, and I do not know what to do with it. I feel the nibbles of panic again and realize that I am afraid. She is quite plainly saying that everything has changed, that nothing will ever be the same again, and more than anything at the moment I seem to want things to stay the same. Change is tugging at me, and I want to hold on to things as they are. I want to sit there, like I've done in the past, just quietly watching her do something whose every step is known to me and holds no unpleasant surprises.

But Dadda is dead. I can't avoid that fact. It makes me shiver, so that clumsily I say, "But you've got Billy and Joe, and Pat-Joe up the road, and Nuala back home for a while. They can run the farm very well, can't they, Granny?"

She looks at me then, with her eyes bright blue with tears, and I know that she won't let me pretend that she'd meant "manage" in that sense. The house, the farm, the animals: all that will run as smoothly as it has ever done, just as she will stand here every morning as she is doing now and has always done, making the cake for breakfast.

But her eyes are telling me the real truth of the meaning in her words. They won't let me escape from the fact that something has changed, something has passed and will never return. Something is lacking and is filling her days with emptiness, despite all the hundred and one things she finds to do. The thought of this void terrifies me, and I want to edge past it, but her grief will not allow me to.

Her hands meet in the bowl. They are making magic in the mix, melding and molding the sticky mass until it becomes as warm and smooth and whole as the soft skin on the insides of her arms. Although she is grief-stricken, her work has rhythm to it which cannot pause until the job is done. Her sorrow darts out here and there above the busy movements of her hands, in soft words of sadness. She divides the warm lump into four pieces, sprinkles them with flour, and flattens them with her hands before placing them on the sheet of iron which I have passed to her. Then she takes a knife and with its point she scores each cake with the shape of a cross. That way they break into four quarters when they're baked.

And all the while, and all the while that follows as she cooks the bacon and the eggs, and warms the plates, and dishes out the food and leaves it to warm, her words grow in number as she tells me this story, which I'll try and tell you for now as best I can, with no interruptions.

✒ Nine

"Poor Michael, where is he now? All the long years I spent with him, and now he is gone. All the days I worked beside him, building this house and growing the land. The childer we brought into the world and cared for and tended, and now half of them gone, over the four seas, forever more. All the long years and now he is gone. And sure he nearly wasn't even my husband at all.

"A stroke of fate it was that brought us together, all those years ago. Wasn't I engaged to be married to Billy Coogan of the Wexford Road? But doesn't God work in mysterious ways, for wasn't poor Billy taken away from me before we'd even named the day to the priest.

"Do y'see, Mary, in those days Ireland was in uproar and chaos. There were no six counties in the north; Ireland was all one country then. There were two governments here: one was the Dail, the government of the people of Ireland, and the other was Dublin Castle, where the English ruled. There was a general election in all Ireland, and the people elected those that they wanted to govern them in the Dail. They elected 130

Republicans out of a total of 180, and sure, God help us, didn't this provoke the fury of the English.

"What did they do? They said that the Dail was an illegal assembly, even though the people of Ireland had voted for it, and they tried to put all those elected men in prison. They had the army here then, harrying and troubling all the people, and so the Republicans formed an army themselves and called it the Volunteer force. Their job was to put a stop to the doings of the British Army, and sure they did their job so well that the English had to come up with another plan.

"Sure the Volunteer force did so well because we were all working to help them, women and little childer, we were their eyes and ears. Billy was a Volunteer and so was poor Michael, and many of the men and lads hereabouts. Those that couldn't join the force helped in other ways, whereas the British Army had no one to help them, but everyone against them, for what right did they have to be here at all anyway?

"So the English government and its generals put their heads together and came up with an idea. They decided to form a new branch of the army, specially to deal with the Irish people. The people called them the Black-and-Tans—they had a special uniform in those colors—and sure weren't they the very lowest of the low of the dregs of English society. Some say they were called after the pack of hunting dogs in Limerick, where they first arrived. But sure, poor dogs act only on instinct; whereas these men acted out of low and vicious cruelty.

"The generals went to the prisons in England and they spoke to the men who were imprisoned there for crimes of violence. They said to them, we will release you from prison if you join the Black-and-Tans. Sure God, didn't the men fall over themselves to join! Then they came over here and they holed up in the barracks in the bigger towns, and they went out and about in armored cars doing whatever evil devilment came into their heads. Murder, torture, burning, and looting, they did it all. And they said they were acting on orders.

"Oh Mary, poor Ireland was in chaos and uproar! Billy Coogan and the likes of him used to plan raids and ambushes, anything to halt the Tans, and the heart in me was near dying every night for fear of their lives. They'd dig a trench across the lane when they heard tell of a convoy planning to come that way, and then they'd hide behind the ditches with heaps of stones to pelt at the soldiers when they came to grief in the trench, and the odd rifle to finish their work for them, if they were lucky.

"Now on this one particular day, there they were, waiting in the ditch for the convoy to pass. But Lord bless us and save us, didn't someone—I've always said it was that shreel of a woman Kitty Maloney, who was always after following the English for whatever bit of a treat she could get out of them—didn't someone anyway tell on them, so that the Black-and-Tans came up on them from behind and let rip with their guns, and wasn't poor Billy killed by a bullet through the brain.

"Ah, poor Billy was killed, but a few of the lads got away over the fields and went into hiding, in the hopes of escaping the reprisals that would surely follow. The English knew that Billy had been courting me, so didn't they come to my poor mother's house, looking for evidence, they said. They were certain sure that we were hiding some of the poor lads that had escaped.

"But sure poor Mammy knew nothing. She had enough to do at that time to keep the place going with Daddy dead, God bless him, and only me and my two young brothers left to run the farm. But the English cared little for that. They came roaring and swaggering into the yard, holding their guns as though they were holding the Holy Sacrament itself, God forgive me. They kicked the poor old dog who was barking at them fit to burst. God help him, didn't they batter his brains out against the yard wall.

"Mammy and I were in the kitchen with Keiran, but Donal was away out in the meadow with the horse, plowing drills. We stood close together and they burst into the house, and never will I forget till the day I die the state they left us in.

"I'd never seen the English so close before. They were not like any of the men I'd ever seen. Their voices didn't seem to use the words of talking; instead they made harsh roars and growlings, like the mad dogs when they're fighting. They strutted and strode about the place so that the whole house seemed to become small somehow. They pelted the thatch down off the roof; looking for suspects, they said. Then didn't they heft the mattresses off the two beds and slit them to pieces with their wicked bayonets. They tore all poor Mammy's bedclothes into ribbons and flitters, and then they fired into the kitchen. They shot bullets into the presses and smashed every stick of crockery, and then they kicked the fire around the room and piled all the cooking pots out into the yard.

"The blood in me was boiling and I was near killed trying to get them to stop, praying and beseeching them, for weren't they destroying everything that we had in the world. Mammy was standing still with little Keiran wrapped to her legs, saying the rosary silently, her lips moving and her eyes blank.

"But by far the worst was yet to come. Didn't one of them find the press with my mother's underclothing in it, all her shifts and the bits of things she was saving for me and I married. Didn't he think he was made up as he dragged them out into the yard on the end of his bayonet. He was roaring and barking, and then didn't his companions join in, roaring and spitting, passing water on them and trailing them around the yard in the muck and the filth, spearing them with their bayonets, waving them round each other's faces, kicking them around with their boots.

"My poor mother never recovered from that day. The heart went out of her after that. The sight of her personal bits of clothing being exposed to such attention shamed her to her very soul, I think. I stopped my pleading and stood by her. I knew there was no point trying to reach them with my words now.

"I held Mammy, and we watched them as they finished their work. They went off to the hay barn next, and turfed out every bit of hay that myself and Donal had near killed ourselves bringing in. They strewed it about the yard until it was so drenched with muck and water that none of it could be saved. Then they attacked the poor fowl and the innocent beasts, God help them; weren't they crying and screaming as the soldiers made away with them, shooting and stabbing and ripping their guts out and streaming their poor innards all over the yard.

"When they'd destroyed everything that their hands came upon, they stood barking at each other as their chests went up and down with their panting. Then one of them ran to where some of the turf lay burning on the ground from the fire, and he speared it with his bayonet and hurled it at the thatch. Of course then they all had to have a go at that and one of them ran and fired what was left of the hay barn too. There was nothing more they could destroy now, except for us.

"But Mammy's rosary must have reached the ear of God, for didn't they just come up to us and spit on us, but that was all they did. Keiran had his eyes closed, and he didn't even open them when he felt the spittle run over his face. They left then, off in a hurry, and we were left alone, in the crackling of the fire.

"We watched the dark smoke billow round the house.

We could not move. It was as though the dark force which had made those devils behave as they did had paralyzed our limbs. I felt in my stomach and in the marrow of my bones. We walked to the gateway then, and turned our heads to Mount Leinster in the distance, and waited for the spirit to return to our limbs. Eventually I bent down and said a prayer for the poor old dog. I couldn't look at his head, but I put my hand on his side. It was still warm.

"Then I started to move about the yard, picking up poor Mammy's underclothes from the shame of the public gaze. I'd a mind to draw some water and make up a fire, to boil some water for to wash them in. When who should come running in at the gate but your grandfather, Michael.

"He was my cousin, and a fair bit older than me, and a more fine upstanding young man you'd travel far to see the likes of. He looked at the house, and his gaze roved over the yard and over the desolation and blood there was everywhere to be seen. Then he walked straight up to me, and with his head held high he said, 'Would you marry me, Molly?' And wasn't it the strange thing that without hesitation, 'I will,' says I.

"So there you are. That is the story of how in one and the same day I lost one man, and found another, and how it came about that Michael was your grandfather.

"He moved in with us, so he did, and he rebuilt the house and filled the place with young beasts in no time at all, it seemed. The chaos in Ireland continued, in murder and bloodshed and economic war, and each Sunday we visited the cross put up to Billy and his comrades on the road out of the barracks. We prayed for peace and prosperity to come to our land, as a fit memorial to those who had died for her. And in our own homes we tried to live in peace, for is it not in each human heart that the seeds of peace must grow, if the world is to be free and prosper?

"Michael worshiped poor Mammy and did all he could to bring brightness down upon her head again. When Donal and Keiran were big enough to run the farm on their own, we moved out and began to build our own place—that's this very same house that we are in now. When it was built, sure Michael couldn't rest himself till we had Mammy moved in with us, and she stayed with us until her dying day.

"Not a day goes by but that I remember the circumstances of our marriage, and I thank God that out of so much wickedness and sorrow a bright hope emerged and stayed with me all these years.

"Ah Michael, you were a good man, fine and true. And how will I manage without you, at all?"

⚘ Ten

Granny finishes her cooking, and the food is dished out, and we sit in silence as the people in the story she has just told slowly fade away. There is nothing I can say.

And then the door opens and everyone comes in, and all is bustle as they sit down and eat the food she's cooked. Not one of them knows what I know, that her heart was bleeding as she cooked it all. She sits on the hearth quietly, getting up now and again to fill the teapot or to pass the plates, and the porridge is eaten, and the rashers and eggs, and the cake is broken and covered in butter and every crumb is swallowed. "Thanks be to God for the fine food," says everyone as they get up from the table.

But no one says "Thank you" to Granny, and the food is all eaten in twenty minutes.

✍ Eleven

It's so strange, not having Dadda in the house. We all called him Dadda when he was alive. Of course Mammy and her brothers and sisters did, and I suppose that all us children did because he was really the head of the house. Dadda, who started the whole thing off, who built the house and brought us all into the world, in one way or another. It was thanks to him that we are all here. And since Granny's story I know how true that is. And why everything that was done around the house and land was done on his say-so. So that it's really strange, him not being here anymore.

I remember one Sunday years ago, when we'd all come home after Mass. We were all in our Sunday best, my uncles stiff and awkward in their suits, me driven to distraction by my frills and gloves and starched petticoats. For devilment, I had thrown myself into his armchair as soon as we got into the kitchen. Then I'd felt my heart sinking as I felt under my behind the rough stiff shape of something. It was his hat, squashed beneath my bum like a cowpat.

I remember everyone shrieking with horror as I drew

it out from under me. "Jaysus, she's after destroying Dadda's good hat!"

"Quick till I see!"

"Sure what'll we tell him?"

I felt the blood leave my head as I slowly realized that the grown-ups who were my uncles and aunts were terrified of him. I realized that he must be truly king of the world if even my uncle Billy stood white and pale with shock, holding the flattened thing in his hands.

I began to cry, terrified of doom and damnation crashing down onto my head, so that when Dadda himself came in, the first thing he saw was me, hot and red and wet with tears. He drew me to him as he sat down in his armchair, and, looking up to see the cause of the trouble, said only, "Ah, sure, give the owld hat a bit of a steam in the kettle there. Whisht, allanah! Lookit, what have I in me pocket?"

I was saved, but my aunts and uncles looked at me strangely as I sat in state on his lap, playing with his fob watch. I realize now that they must have felt angry at seeing me get off so lightly when they'd suffered greatly from his anger in the past. They were still his children, and he was a big man, and he'd ruled his family with a firm back and a rod of iron and very few words.

Now I see that he must have had to, with so many mouths depending on him for food, so much land to coax into life with just his own arms and back. When I knew him, the hardest days were over for him, for he had three grown sons to help him then. And I was his grandchild, his hope for the future, so he was gentle with me. I saw a different side of him to the one his children had seen. I wonder if, when Mammy has grandchildren, whether she will show them another side of herself to the one she has shown us, her children?

Dadda spoke very little, I remember. Granny would always be telling us some story, or cheerily singing through the day, noticing the comings and goings of the birds and the trees or the progress of the cattle across the near meadow. But Dadda was a silent man, and he used words sparingly.

I have spent hours alone with him, following him like a small shadow, linked to him by the love of horses which he gave to me. I have crouched next to him on the ground and listened to his hands as they ran over the long, taut legs of a limping colt, searching for the place that caused the red-hot pain to swell. I have heard his hands running over the swollen flanks of his pregnant mares, soothing and comforting, and I've seen the ears of the horses flick back and forth in conversation with him, in silence.

In silence too he taught me how to become fluent in handling the complex harnesses, the straps and chains, the hooks and buckles, so that I could harness a horse to the plow or to the trap before I could cook a meal. All the work on the farm was done by his teams of Shires and Clydesdales, creatures so tall that I could walk beneath them without stooping to loop the linking chains from the bellyband to the shafts. And he loved those beasts in silence, respecting their labor which kept his land prosperous at a time when Ireland was cast down into poverty and hunger.

Many a time I have walked through the near meadow with a bucket of oats in my hand, and I have seen the beauty of horses gliding around us, swimming belly-high in the morning mist. I have seen Dadda speak with them in the same silent language that they use, almost as though he was thanking them for allowing us to place the bridles over their heads, that we might use their labor all the day long. I always used to believe that they'd never have allowed this to happen, that they'd have flung themselves off into the mist and freedom if it wasn't for the fact that every morning without fail, Dadda would thank them wordlessly and with great respect as they stood in a circle round us, with their heads held high and their breath quietly fluting on the misty air.

I shared many quiet and busy times with him. I know that the Dadda I knew was different to the one my mammy knew, and the one that all her brothers and sisters feared. How strange it is, that people are each of them many different people, rolled up inside one body.

Now that Dadda is dead, I have no more silent busy times, and Billy, Joe, and Pat-Joe have no one to rule them anymore. I am scared, because now I keep hearing Billy talking about tractors, bringing home brochures, discussing the merits of this one or that one. I want to scream at him, no, no, leave everything as it was in Dadda's day, with the clean warm stables and the massive gentle creatures who are our friends. But I know that Billy wants a big, loud filthy machine, pissing oil and belching fumes, because one of those can do the work of ten horses in a quarter of the time. I am terrified at how quickly things are changing.

✣ Twelve

I wonder what happens to people when they die.

Dadda's body is in the churchyard, under a clean new stone. We will see it when we go to Mass on Sunday. But where is the person who was Dadda? His absence is everywhere, in the stables, beside the rows of harness hanging from their pegs, between the upturned shafts of the trap, which is lying like a ghost behind the hay barn now that he's not here to harness it each morning. They use the Ford Popular to go everywhere now, except to the creamery in the mornings, and I'm sure they only continue to use the creamery cart because the churns won't fit in the backseats of the car.

I look at the trap and I am full of my favorite memories of all: the days Dadda would take me with him to go to the market and do the messages in town. It was a great thing to be with him in the trap, all fresh and gleaming, and to be bowling along on the smooth tires, watching the bright shafts as they were brushed by the silvery strands of the horse's tail. She was the gray mare, whose soft eyes had made her Dadda's favorite, and she was always the one he chose to take him to town for the fair.

I'd sit up on the front, next to Dadda, and he'd allow me to hold the reins until we got to the Carlow Cross. I'd sit there so pleased and proud and silent, watching the horizon between the mare's flicking ears or her round ripe bum rolling from side to side in its two cheeks in front of me. Sometimes the arch of her tail would lift and sweep my legs with stings, but I'd never flinch. Sometimes she'd fart, and sometimes the round, puckered place under her tail would slowly swell and turn inside out, and out would come the neat molded plops of her business. I would watch this procedure with fascination. I thought she was a great one to be able to do her business at a fast trot, never slowing down, dropping the neat precise little bundles.

The lanes and roads were not tarmacked then, and the furrows caused by many journeys were digging the lanes lower and lower on either side of its central ridge. They carved it ever more precisely between the ditches which tumbled upward to the roof of the sky in a thick tangle of growing things. Some of these things were delicious to eat, if ever you had a mind to when walking along beside them, and if you knew which ones. The grass bordering the lane had a long feel to it, lush and lovely, and the mare tossed her head at it as we slowed down at the crossroads and Dadda took the reins off me. "Ah no, ah no," he'd say as he clipped at the reins to urge her past her temptation.

When we got to town we'd tether the mare in amongst the ranks of other ponies and traps, in the shade of the trees down the middle of the long main street. Then, before we went to look at the pens of horses and calves, we'd go and do the messages, me with the lists, Dadda with the bundles. These, whether they were brack or bacon, vegetables or methylated spirits, were always wrapped carefully in nice brown paper and tied with skillful twine.

The things we'd buy would be few, precise, and simple, but the purchase of each one would be a great event for me, the visiting grandchild from England, being scrutinized and questioned by all the shopkeepers. They were a talkative, quick-moving sort of people, and my grandfather in his big coat and loud boots seemed to dwarf not only them, but the whole of their shops as he entered, dark in the doorway, and removed his hat. His body was huge and slow, as was his voice, but I could tell they all respected him from the way they took his huge red hand, with the coarse white hairs upon it, into their small slim ones and shook it courteously.

They bustled about us in their brown aprons, darting me quick probing glances, as though spying out signs of a shrewd corruption. Sometimes they deliberately misunderstood my prim English voice as I carefully and with great embarrassment gave them the orders from Granny. It was all a bit of a trial for me, until Dadda moved near me and showed me by his close presence that I was doing fine, and that he was proud of me. It was as though his presence bestowed upon me the right to be me, and to be comfortable.

When at last I'd reached the end of the list, the shop-keepers would say, "And now, Michael, will you have a glass?" And he'd say, "Well now, how about a few bis-cuits?" and the shopkeepers would wink at me and at him, and they'd weigh out some of those Jacobs' biscuits with the soft pink stuff on top that is covered with little splinters of dry coconut. I'd lean against the counter munching them until he'd finished his stout and I my mineral.

We'd walk back to the trap with our bundles and stow them under the seat in the cool. Then would follow a couple of hours of silence for me while he walked around the calf pens, murmuring with some of the other men, comparing prices and the setup of the animals. I could hardly bear to wait for the moment when at last he'd walk to look at the horses.

I was captivated as they were led out, wild eyed on the ends of their reins, heads rearing up, tails arched, spinning and backing up, being run through the streets to show off their paces, their demeanor, and their strength. Sometimes he'd spend a couple of hours there, just looking and taking his time, while men came up to him and tried to find out which horses he favored espe-cially. He was famous for having a great eye for the horses, and his word was usually taken as law.

That's how I'll remember him best, with me swinging on the pens beside him, looking over the horses while he puffed at a Players. It was the only time I ever used to see him standing idle, but I know that his eyes and brain were busy, scrutinizing and measuring.

I never realized how much I used to rely on his presence, how easily he made me feel at home and comfortable, until he was gone. Now, in the afternoons I shuffle about the yard aimlessly, and I do not know where I belong. My memories of him bring him closer to me than a cold white gravestone ever could. He was an ordinary man, but he was a hero too. I know that now.

❧ Thirteen

Daddy is always so smart and dapper in his suit and tie, walking around the yard with his hands in the pockets of his pressed trousers. Billy and Joe are huge men beside him, and seem much more slow in their movements. Their boots scrape along the concrete in big steps, compared to the light quick movements of his shiny brown shoes.

He's often not here in the daytime, just like he was at home and going to work every day. Sometimes I ask him, "Where are you going today, Daddy?" and he says, "I can't tell you that, because if I did you'd know as much as I do, and that would never do." Then he laughs and catches someone's eye, and they both carry on laughing.

How he confuses me! When he fancies talking to me about Ireland, he doesn't mince his words. But other times he deliberately keeps things from me. As though deliberately trying to slow down the passage of time, trying to keep me a child.

He often tinkers with the Ford Popular, and Billy and

Joe stand by him, looking at him with respect as he talks of tappets and valves and oil levels.

Granny always serves his food first at mealtimes, and gives him the juiciest slice of ham or the best cuts of beef. His table manners are neat and precise. He always cuts his slice of bread into four pieces, putting each one delicately into his mouth. My uncles tear mouthfuls from a whole slice, and so do I. Mammy says, "There isn't a better man in the whole world than your daddy. He worked so hard when he had nothing to give you a house to live in and food to eat."

He came over to England barefoot when he was thirteen years old, and his determination got him a job when work was so scarce. He went to night school after work to get more qualifications. He traveled across London on his bicycle to get to work in the dawn, and then at nights back again to his classes.

Mammy says that there is nothing he couldn't have been if he'd only had the opportunities that some have had. He was a wireless operator in the war. He can mend the big radio when it breaks. He can mend anything that goes wrong. He mends our bikes and the car, and he mends our shoes too. He has a last and all the proper tools.

He doesn't know much anymore about how to run a farm, and he watches the animals from afar, with a kind of distant respect.

At home in England, I have never seen him with a

drink in his hand. He says that alcohol is a dreadful curse, and it ruined his father and has been the ruination of the Irish in England. But here in the kitchen at night, he often has a glass of Guinness with Billy and Joe, Mammy and Nuala. His face becomes rosy with jokes, and his eyes twinkle with blueness.

He never used to hit us when we were small, but now he takes a stick to all of us when we back-answer him, me and John more often than Anne. He used to answer all my questions as I squatted beside him in the garden. But now he is more confusing. He tells me many things as though I were an adult, but some other things he brushes from him, walking away from me with a flick of his hand.

✒ Fourteen

The mornings are all right. I spend them as I've always done, helping Granny as she does all the morning jobs, outside in the first breath of the day. Anne has never joined in with this work; she usually goes somewhere with Daddy. John usually stays with the men, bringing in the cows from the field and hanging round the cow house while they're milked. He's too small to carry a full pail of milk from the cow house to the churns outside by the wall where they are strained through muslin. But Billy lets him carry armfuls of hay to the racks at the cows' heads, so they've something to munch while they're being milked. Mammy and Nuala help with the milking like they always used to do when they lived here, sitting on three-legged stools with their heads against the warm flanks of the cows, gossiping peacefully.

I begin by cleaning the range around the fire with a goose wing, sweeping the ashes from every corner and cranny, doing a good job too, with one eye out for the scanning lurch of Granny's critical gaze. I kneel on the stones around the fire, polishing them by spitting and sweeping with the stiff feathers. Sometimes I test my voice by leaning back and trilling up the chimney, sending the clearest notes I can find to bounce up the rough stones to the sky in the hole at the top.

Granny hefts down the huge iron pot, filled with creamy-scented meal, from the hook which suspends it all night long to cook slowly beneath the stars. She says, "Will you get down from there now, Mary, and cover your knees, and be a good girl and help me with this."

She has the pot on the kitchen floor, stirring the thick, billowing mash with a smooth stick. She holds the stick in both of her hands, her little hands whose skin is loose, white, and transparent as the honesty flowers when they whiten. Her little body is always sensibly wrapped up, like one of her parcels, in a navy blue overall with a pattern of tiny flowers. She makes these aprons in the winter evenings and stores them in the press beneath the wireless set. That way she never has to suffer the shame of starting a new day in the grubby one she's taken off the night before.

She replaces the lid of the pot, and we walk across the kitchen floor. I walk backward, holding the pot handle in both my hands, keeping a sharp lookout behind me to make sure I'm not leading us into collision with the table, or with the forms, or with the crafty bulbs of the big wooden feet of Dadda's armchair.

We make it to the door without mishap, and out we go, avoiding the iron ingot propping it open, which would love to stub our toes. With dog tails pluming and weaving around us, we shuffle across the yard. The dogs live outdoors here, curling up at night in the hay barn, where they have fine sport keeping down the rats. They don't get fed special meals, only the scraps of our food at the end of every meal. But they crave human company, and all day long they are around you if you go out the house door. They follow us now with their noses tweaked by the warm scent of the mash as we set the pot down by the wall next to a row of pails which stand unevenly on their last legs. They are no longer serviceable as milk pails, being beaten and crusty, with a few holes here and there, and when they become too old and useless to serve as feed pails they'll become store boxes for scraps of rusting metal, old nails, ends of rope, nuts and bolts, and so on, lined up inside the stable wall.

But now we tip the mealy mash into each of them, with the dogs keeping a respectful distance which doesn't fool Granny, for she covers the pot with a lid, and then we carry the pails toward the chicken house. Granny carries one under each arm, for they have no handles. She sets one down, craftily, behind where the door will be when she opens it, and she undoes the latch. With shrieks and eruptions of fluttering wings and beating air and stamping feet, the chickens and ducks swoop out into the yard.

"Cheek, chck chck chck!" soars the liquid voice of Granny as she walks up toward the hay barn in her old boots, throwing handfuls of mash around her as she goes, in a cloud of feathers and uproar. Carefully singling out the weakest birds for special, secret handfuls, she soon empties the pail and bangs it against a post to get rid of the last globs clinging to the bottom of it. Back she comes toward me, and into the henhouse with her empty pail to crawl around on the sharp-smelling carpet of straw and chicken shit, feeling with her hands into the darkest corners, singing loudly to scare away, oh lord, the rats. I would never do that, as shivers trickle up and down my back, not even for the alabaster shells of the duck eggs.

"There's a grand duck egg for Billy's breakfast," she says with satisfaction, and pops it into her bucket with all the brown and speckled hens' eggs. "Mary, sure will you look out for them cats," she says to me as I stand idling, tickling my cheek with a piece of straw. I look down and meet the unblinking collective gaze of a row of skinny malinkies, tortoiseshell and sweet as sugar in picture books but here as sharply spitting and red of tooth and claw as rats. I clench my fists and stamp, but they are not fooled, not they, and I feel my face go red with rage as I roar at them, "Get away, go on, get off!" And I stamp and prance in front of the full meal pails to keep them away.

Luckily for me, at that moment Joe comes out of the cow house, his arms tight and corded from the weight of the milk pails he is carrying. As he walks, a few little drips of milk leap over the tops of the pails and land on the ground, and in one gauzy movement all the cat creatures are seated round these drips, delicately lapping.

"Sure, the poor craythers have to fill their bellies like the rest of us," says Granny kindly as she comes out of the henhouse, her pail now full of eggs, wiping her free hand on her overall. At the sound of her heavy boots all the cats evaporate back into the shadows, to emerge around the churns where the milk, which Joe has tipped in, drips in periodic droplets from the frayed ends of the muslin down onto the ground. "It's a grand day," he says as he passes us, kicking the shit from his boots. At each metallic scrape of his soles, a pent leap trembles down the backs of the wild cat bodies as they sip each dangerous tongueful.

Then on we go, gathering the full pails in passing, Granny and I, she calling, "It's a grand day, Billy, thanks be to God," as we pass the cow house. On to the calf house and the heavy latch and the gentle warm breath waiting behind, eyes rolling watchfully at Granny's stick, which she waves from its place behind the door.

"Back, back wit' ye, ye little divils!" she growls, her voice fierce for these youngsters, and we heave the pails in and wade through the soft bodies to their trough, she beating back their heads which try to plunge into the pails before they're tipped into the trough. I love the feeling of their heads nudging my back and thighs, and I pass my face close to their bodies to catch their smell and warmth, and the sweet pink rippling of their muzzles as they quest forward to the food.

We stand for a minute, watching them eat, and she praises their strong young bodies with satisfied little pats of her hand on their flanks. "Grand lads, grand lads altogether," she croons, and then off we go once more, taking their water buckets to fill at the well higher up the yard. Sometimes I run ahead of her while she pauses to latch the door, and I heave back the large, mossy circle of wood that covers the well.

I love to gaze down into the silent crystal which glitters at the bottom of the dark and mossy walls. Such a long way down! So clear and cold, and silent with its secrets, the water flickers down there in the dark, fringed with ferns. But Granny always panics seeing me there, and to her I am nothing more than a child as she shrieks, "Mary! Will you get back from there before the bogeyman gets you! Jesus, Mary, and Joseph, how many times do you have to be told!"

She grabs a rope and grumbles at my wickedness as she flings a pail down the well, bracing herself to stop it banging against the walls and spilling on its way up. I can't answer her back. I have never ever back-answered my granny in my life. I'm bursting to tell her that I can be trusted not to tip myself down the well, that I'm not a baby anymore. But I don't know how to talk to her, so I keep silent, and capably cling to the full pail she passes to me.

I carry it, leaning over it to dare it to spill a drop, to the calf-house door, where I wait, like a good girl, for her to come and undo the latch, still grumbling at me over her full pail. I stand back to let her in first, so that she can place her pail in the nice smooth indentation in the thick straw where it was standing before. Then I edge round and place mine in the trickier place, leaning in a fork where two timbers rise out of the straw side by side.

And so out we go again, into the milky light of a bit of sunshine seeping through the even silent pallor of the early sky. And I help her with the breakfast in the house, and with the washing up. I know what to do in the mornings. I just accompany Granny in her work, like I've always done. At least it's safe, and I know what to do. I am her good girl, Mary. But when I feel restless and agitated, I don't know what to say to her. And I don't know how to tell her that I can be trusted now with the fire and with the well. As far as she's concerned, I'm just the same as I've always been.

But the afternoons are terribly hard to get through.

❧ Fifteen

Mammy says:

"You're not to go out into the fields, bothering Billy and Joe. You're too big now to go tagging along after them. They have work to do, sure.

"Don't go anywhere near them horses. You can't trust them an inch. Watch their back legs or you'll be killed. Poor Dadda had his leg smashed once.

"Pull down your skirt and cover your knees, you bold hussy.

"Keep away from the mare. She'd kill you soon as look at you, and her with her foal to protect.

"Don't be climbing up in that hay barn. If you fall, you'll be killed.

"Go back upstairs and take off them jeans. Sure God's truth why do I have to be telling you. Why can't you wear a dress like a decent young girl?

"Keep out of them stables. You'll be covered in muck."

I'm drowning in her orders. But I manage to defy her whenever I can. I climb up into the soft hay in the barn, on my own or sometimes with John. We have some great games, John and me, rolling about in the hay high up near the roofbeams, pushing each other down the steep drop where last year's hay is nearly all used up. Giggling and out of breath, we hide from each other, burying ourselves in the sweet, dry-smelling heaps, scratching ourselves on the dry stalks of last summer's grasses. We smother ourselves in the hot scents of other dusty, pollen-laden summer days. And we terrify ourselves and each other with tales of the rats, who live in a mazy kingdom of tunnels and flashing eyes right below where we sit.

When John has things of his own to do, I sit up there on my own, watching all the comings and goings in the yard below me. They have nothing to do with me and I watch them from the outside. I bury my face in the soft, rich hay and feel totally alone.

Sometimes I pass the long aimless hours by reading, my head stuffed full of other people's lives, or else sometimes I draw, losing myself completely as I try to catch the trees against the house or the chair in front of the fire. And sometimes I try to write the torment I am feeling in the margins of my sketchbook. But I can't describe it properly and often I just end up crying, I feel so sorry for myself. And then I'm scared that someone else will see what I have written, and I run away to hide my book.

Granny is oblivious. She says, "Sure isn't Mary the

fine scholar, always with her nose in a book. She'll be winning prizes for the grand drawings she does be doing, and for the brains she has in her head."

I must be an alien to her, with my books and my pencils. Here, no one ever reads or writes or draws. So why do I? Where do I get it from? All they do here is talk. Talking, talking; morning, noon, and night they are always talking. And I am silent. When I do say something, my voice is flat and awkward with the dead vowels of London, and it sounds so weird in among the rising falling song of the way they talk here.

Anne goes off with Daddy nearly every day. She doesn't ever help with things around the house, so I hardly ever see her except at mealtimes. She loves getting dressed in her best clothes and taking trips to Kilkenny with Daddy. She's almost a stranger to me, my own sister. When she is around the house, she's always bothering me, nosing about me when I'm trying to read or draw, picking up my books and sneering at them. And John can go off with my uncles anytime he wants. They never turn him away, like they do with me. I'd love to see my cousins, Siobhan, Carmel, and Orla, but they are Pat-Joe's only children, so they have to help him every day during the school holidays around his farm. It seems that I'm the only one for miles around who has nowhere to fit in, no place to belong.

I feel cold inside my skin. And so lonely. No one ever touches me, except for Mammy when she slaps me. I am too big now to curl up on anyone's lap. I don't know how to leave this silent, tortured shell of solitude. Mammy says keep away from the horses, but their silence and slow-breathing warmth is the only thing I have in this whole wide world to give me any feeling of comfort.

❧ Sixteen

I'm sitting in the haggard at the back of the house, where the vegetables are grown and where the laundry is hung to dry over the bushes and along the gaily flapping line. It is peaceful here in the quiet time of the day when all the men have returned to work in the fields. Nuala and Mammy are off visiting with Anne and John, and Daddy has gone off to see a house in Kilkenny. Prince is lying here beside me, with his eyes closed but with one ear up on guard, ready to pick up any sound which will make him spring into action. The air is flickering with insects, and sometimes Prince snaps with a click of his teeth and swallows an unwary fly who dives too near his nose.

I have been drawing a horse in my book for Dadda. She is a gray mare. Her ears are pricked and sharp with alertness. The broad plane of her forehead spreads wide to the ridges of her huge dark eyes. The long line of her face ends at the flaring of her nostrils and the soft, fluttering velvet of her nose. I could pat the broad swell of her cheek. There is a taut line of muscle along the arc of her neck. Her mane is lifted from the neck to crest like a breaker before falling in glorious waves upon her shoulders. Dadda would be pleased by the strong rounded muscles on her chest, the four slim taut legs, the springy fetlocks, and the polished hooves. Powerful muscles ripple under the swell of her rump.

More than anything I would like a horse of my own, like this beautiful dream mare. I would ride then, alone down the laneways and over the fields to the far horizons, with no one else for company except maybe Prince, trotting at our heels.

But now Granny is calling me from the back-kitchen window, and I must go.

She meets me at the house door with her sleeves rolled up and a sense of urgent purpose about her.

"Mary, the little sow is after starting her labor, and I'm thinking she'll be needing our assistance. She's struggling and near killed with the strain. Will you fill the clean enamel basin with some warm water and bring a cake of soap along with it to the sow house? Hurry now, while I go and get some sacks."

There is no one about but Granny and me, and I hurry to do as she bids me. I carry the basin and soap, and a towel as well, along to the sow house. Granny is in there, on the floor, kneeling by the great bulk of the sow, who is lying on the ground grunting in pain. Granny's little freckled hand is feeling along the coarse skin of the sow's side, pressing gently here and there to feel what is going on inside. The sow's head is stretched back and her whole body shudders now and again. Under her skin, it ripples in churning spasms.

"Set down the basin, Mary," says Granny, "and pass me the cake of soap." She dips her hands in the water, splashing it up her arms, and then she soaps them from wrist to elbow, building up a good leather. She places one arm on the backside of the sow, crooning softly to her.

"It's my opinion one of them bonhams is turned the wrong way round," she explains. "It'll be blocking up the exit for the others and sure, the poor old craythur will be killed trying to get them out."

Her hand goes under the tail of the sow, where the huge red-and-purple fanny pulses and gapes like a living creature. Then she inserts first her fingers, then her hand and then her wrist, right up inside it.

I am awestruck, but Granny seems to know exactly what to do. The sow is screaming at first, but now she begins a rhythmic grunting as Granny slowly pushes her arm higher up inside her. The sow's little eye is glinting darkly as Granny slowly revolves her arm, doing something with her fingers deep inside. "Come along now, you little divil," she says.

She slowly withdraws her arm, and, as her hand comes out, a bloody little bundle flops out with it onto the straw, like something wrapped in red cellophane. It lies motionless, with bits of blood and tissue dripping from it, and Granny begins to rub it briskly with some sacking. It is a perfect baby pig, white and clear, very pale with its perfect little snout and four neat, creamy, almost transparent little trotters. As I watch, it begins to squeak with all its might, and it seems to fill with color under my eyes, so that its skin becomes suffused with pink, until it wobbles to its feet and starts rummaging for its mother's teats.

"A fine strong lad," says Granny, sounding pleased. "Wait till we see now whether we've removed the cause of the obstruction." The sow's grunts become louder, and her fanny opens like a big strong mouth, and out comes another bundle like the first. "Wipe him down," says Granny, and I do so, rubbing the sac away to reveal another perfect little body which starts to struggle to its feet immediately and skitters squeaking toward its mother's source of food and warmth.

We stay there until thirteen have come out one by one. Two of them stay white even after we've rubbed them, and then they turn a blue-gray color. The life does not come flooding into them; they have been born dead. Granny wraps them in some sacking. And when we leave the sow there are eleven babies fighting for her teats, which swell in two distended rows along the length of her belly as she grunts and noses them.

The rest of that warm and drowsy afternoon I wander about the yard, poking my nose in at all the houses where there are baby animals. I sit down in the straw with the baby calves, only a couple of days old, some of them, and so perfectly clean, smelling so fresh and sweet, and already so strong. If you hold out your hand to them, they grasp your fingers in their thick, strong tongues and suck them against the roof of their mouths, dragging them against their toothless upper gums. Their tongues are rough and rasp your skin. This is how, later on, we teach them to take milk from a bucket, by sticking our fingers in the milk, raising them to their mouths so that they suck them, and then lowering them back into the bucket while they're still sucking. In time, the little things get the hang of curling the milk around their tongues unaided, so that they can suck it up and drink. I love the smell of their coats, and I bury my face in them.

Young creatures all around: little chicks cheeping and panicking after their mothers, kittens tumbling and flittering over tangled heaps of rope, the chestnut mare with her foal in the field. But never before have I seen anything actually being born. I've never seen that effort, and the perfection of the newly born creatures, and the mystery. This is how things continue. It's the most ordinary thing in the world. Every second, some new creature is being born. But it's also a miracle, and no one can explain how it is done. I feel so glad that I've seen it, and that I was able to be of some use to Granny. I'm amazed at how quietly and confidently she knew what to do, and where the trouble lay, and that she let me see it.

So when Daddy turns in at the gateway in the Ford Popular, I run up to him excitedly. I feel sure he'll be

pleased to hear about the sow and her babies; he used to
enjoy walking round with Dadda and me sometimes,
looking at the newborn calves. Bubbling with my news,
I rush up to him, calling out as I go, "Daddy! The sow
has had eleven babies, and I helped Granny with her
and saw it all!"

But then I notice that his face, which had turned to
me in interest at first, is avoiding mine. His eyes are wa-
vering away from me, as though he is embarrassed
about something. "Don't be talking that way, Mary," he
says. And then he goes into the house, leaving me
standing there. He's rejected me. What have I done
wrong? Alone and awkward suddenly, standing in the
yard, I just don't know.

❧ Seventeen

In the mornings, when the men come back from the creamery, they bring the mail with them. They collect it from the post office next door. They give all the letters to Granny to open, but none of them is ever addressed to her. On the envelopes it says, "Mr. Michael Kelly" (that is Dadda) or "Mr. William Kelly (Mick)" (that is Uncle Billy). Sometimes, some of them are for Nuala, from America, and they are written in the same way: "Miss Nuala Kelly (Mick)." They put "Mick" in brackets, to show that it's Dadda's house that they're meant for. Because here, houses don't have names or numbers like they do in England. So letters just have someone's name on the envelope, and then the name of the village.

I notice how even though Dadda is dead, all the letters are addressed to him, in one way or another. But it is Granny who is given them to open. She puts on her glasses with the thick, dark rims, and she is in charge. She gives Nuala any letters that are addressed to her, and then the rest she carefully opens with a knife. She works slowly, smoothing the paper flat upon the table before holding it in both hands and reading silently. If the letter is a bill, she takes the old Oxo tin out of the press and carefully counts out notes or coins, and then gives them to Billy, saying, "Make sure you pay this tomorrow now, Billy."

When she's read the letters, she carefully folds them up again and replaces them in their envelopes. She puts them into an old leather handbag that has lost its handle and puts it in the press. Then she takes off her glasses and snaps them into their case and puts it on top of the press, next to the wireless.

I find this a most curious thing. Granny is still alive, so you'd think that the letters would all be addressed to her, now that Dadda is dead. But no, still it's "Mr. Michael Kelly," or "Mr. William Kelly (Mick)." It is as though Granny does not exist.

And yet it is Granny who is the center of the house, Granny with her spectacles who is in charge. Everyone here knows this, but it is never put in writing.

✑ Eighteen

As I run down the stairs today, the first thing I hear is Nuala's voice, singing. She has a lovely voice, and she is making a song out of boiling up some laundry. "Oh glory be to God and all the blessed saints," she trills. "But the fire is sm-o-king BAD!" Her voice has filled the morning with gaiety!

As I move around the kitchen, she's talking to Mammy. She talks fast, and her voice is full of laughter, and they are lifting boiling pots of clothes down off the fire. She is giggling, and so is Mammy—and this is a most unusual sound for me to hear.

Nuala is saying that she has to go into Kilkenny today to pick up some sacks of cement. These are going to be used to build a kind of stand, or cradle, just inside the yard wall near the gateway, to stand a huge diesel tank on. This tank will be for fuel, for the tractor when it comes. Somehow, I have to accept the arrival of this tractor, because it seems it's definitely going to happen.

She asks me if I'd like to go with her, to help her to load the sacks into the backseat of the Ford Popular. I say yes, that would be lovely, just for the ride.

So later, we set off. Nuala holds the steering wheel with one hand, and her other arm is across the back of my seat. She asks me the odd question, and when I answer her, she looks at me in such a way that I know she is listening to every word I say. Her thick hair is hanging loose, like it does when she goes off to a dance in the evenings or to meet some of her friends in Kilkenny. She's wearing her dogtooth check suit with the short little jacket with three big black buttons on it, and the straight skirt which definitely shows her knees.

We ride along with the sun flashing through the windscreen, and Nuala's merry voice makes me feel excited, as though we are off on an adventure. We have a puncture at one point, but Nuala doesn't even mind about that. "Damn the machine to hell!" she says cheerfully, and jumps out to get the jack and the spare wheel and the wheel brace. Then she insists that *I* change the wheel.

"But I don't know how," I protest, blushing, feeling scared in case, after all, she is trying to make me feel small. "But sure God, aren't I here to show you how?" she laughs, and gets me at it, down on the flaky, dry earth of the lane.

"Every woman should know how to change a wheel," she says. "That way, she doesn't have to hang around waiting for some eejit of a man to rescue her!" And we have a lot of fun as she carefully goes through the procedure of undoing the nuts, taking off the old wheel and putting on the new one, tightening the nuts in the right order. Her hands are strong looking, even though they're small, and the nails are beautifully manicured with clear polish on them. All her movements are careful, and if she makes a mistake and the jack comes crashing down—which it does the first time she tries to get it up—she doesn't get all hot and bothered, but just starts talking to it cheerfully and with menace until it is sorted out. When I think how Mammy would have turned something like that into a hysterical drama, I'm amazed that they are sisters, they're so different!

When it is all done, and I am flushed with the effort of tightening the nuts and pleased as well, she puts her arm round me and laughs, looking at my eyes. "Sure, isn't it the great pair of workers we are!" she says as the sunlight ripples in her hair.

As we carry on our way, she asks me have I been to any dances lately. I am quite surprised at this question. Doesn't she know what Mammy is like? I tell her that Mammy won't let me out of the house. There is a lot of bitterness in my voice. Nuala looks straight ahead, making a few little nods. Then she sighs, and her face and voice are so serious that they are almost sad.

"Mary," she says, "it's terrible hard to know how to bring up your children in a foreign country."

My resentment is itching at my throat. "But I'm not a child!" I'm almost shouting. "And what's wrong with going out for a dance now and again? She won't even let me go out with my friends on Saturday afternoons to look round the shops! I mean, what's wrong with doing that?"

Nuala is gazing ahead at the road. She doesn't say anything for a while, and then she asks, "Have you many friends over there?"

"Yes, loads," I say, with my jaw stiff, but I can see her turning her head to me, and her greeny-brown eyes look so kind.

I blush and lower my head so that my hair covers my face. "No, I haven't," I say, and am surprised at how relieved I feel, telling her the truth. I lean my head back against the seat and carry on. "Well, I've got people I can talk to in the dinner hour, you know, and go to games with, but no one I can be that close to, really."

Nuala is silent for a while again, and then she asks quietly, "Are you a bit afraid of them, like, the girls at your school?"

"I suppose I am, a bit," I reply, my voice low.

I turn my head and look out of the window, my heart pounding in my temples. Nuala is easy to tell the truth to, but it hurts, even so, to be back there in England in my thoughts, at this moment. I see the ridged lane ahead of us as we bounce along slowly. We haven't seen a single vehicle on it so far: no cars, and not even a horse and cart. I think of the rushing, fume-filled streets at home.

A muscle is tightening in Nuala's cheek. I know that she might understand, if I can only gather my courage to talk to her. I swallow. "You see, Nuala," I begin, "the thing is, I *know* that it's a foreign country for Mammy, but for me, it's like . . . I mean . . . well, you know, I've always lived there. It's where I have to go to school, and it's where I have to live. And all the other girls there, well, their parents let them . . . I mean . . . they . . . well, they can go out, and they can wear what they like . . . they can even buy their own clothes . . . some of them have Saturday jobs . . . but Mammy and Daddy, they don't let me do anything! Anything at all! Literally!"

I fling myself back in my seat, feeling hopeless. The memory of all that I have to go back to makes me want to cry. It's impossible to make Nuala see what I mean. And she's Mammy's sister, after all, and for all I know, she'll go straight to Mammy when we get back from Kilkenny and tell on me. But she does seem nearer in age to me than to Mammy . . . That makes no difference, though, really. Mammy *is* her sister.

But I've never told *anyone* these things before. Suddenly, I'm frightened that something awful will happen to me, now that I've said them.

But then I feel her hand on the back of my neck, playing with my hair where it grows from the bottom of my head. Her fingers are light and cool, and her touch is so gentle. I feel her fingertips skimming my skin like cool drops of water, and now she is pressing harder, molding the tight bands of muscle on either side of my neck bone. I feel tense; no one ever touches me. But as her fingers carry on, firmly and yet so gently, I feel the tension begin to flow away from me. I keep my head lowered, because I'm too shy to look at her. I'm not used to having anyone touch me like this. It is so nice that I feel myself begin to blush. Oh damn, damn, damn!

Where does this blush come from, and why do I have absolutely no control over it? I feel myself stiffen in confusion. It's no good; I'll have to pull away from her! I can't stand this confusion of feeling. But she takes her hand away first, and now I'm disappointed. If only it could have gone on forever. She must have felt me go stiff. Is she disappointed in me? I feel so hopeless, so useless at knowing how to communicate. Have I lost her again?

She has put both her hands on the steering wheel. Her face is serious. What is she thinking? A living human being sitting next to me, and I haven't a clue what she is thinking. She screws up her face in a wry little smile and sighs. And then, at last, she speaks.

"Well, Mary," she is saying, "sure I have no easy answers for you, and that's the truth. But try not to be too hard on your mammy." So, she *is* taking her side after all! I might have known. Oh, I feel hopeless, hopeless. What's she saying now? "And don't be too hard on yourself, either." I look at her, surprised and puzzled. She is smiling at me now as she continues. "Try not to be forever wishing that you were like those other girls.

You're all right as you are, Mary Maeve O'Reilly, so you are!"

I'm blushing again, because she seems to be saying that she likes me, but I'm irritated as well, because she doesn't seem to have understood how *lonely* I am over there, at school in England. "When all's said and done," she's continuing, "you've a real opportunity there to be better than any of them. You've an opportunity to try and understand them, and to try to understand your mammy, and to be yourself at the end of it all. Then you might find that they'll be fighting over each other to be *your* friend. But you'll have to be strong, oh, you will that. Stronger than any of them."

She sighs again. And I am irritated still. Doesn't she realize that I don't want to be *better* than any of them, I just want to be like them? And I want them to like me! It's all right for *her* to say, "Oh, you've just got to be strong!" What's the point of being strong when you've got no friends and can't get out of the house?

I sit in silence as we draw into Kilkenny. I can still feel the touch of her hand on my skin and deep inside the muscles of my neck. Nuala touched me, and as I frown in annoyance at her last words, I try to hold on to that thought. She touched me, and she did listen to me, and I am grateful for that, at least.

So I giggle with her as she swears at the car, trying to park it, and at her handbag when she drops it, getting out of the car. And when she's paid for the sacks of cement I brace myself to help her carry them into the car. But she's already asked the men to do it for her. As they stow them into the backseat, I look at her inquiringly. And she smiles and touches my neck again.

✒ Nineteen

They've started building the base for the diesel tank, and I've been spending more time with the horses.

I've been going into the stables and breathing in their scent in gulps, and polishing and tidying the tacklings. No one does this anymore, now that Dadda has gone. Billy and Joe are going to buy a Fordson-Major, they've decided, the week after next. They're keeping on the horses until after the harvest, and then they're going to sell them all, except for the gray mare who was Dadda's favorite, because she's getting old now. They say they won't get a good price for them all, because everyone is mad to get tractors. Horses are not wanted anymore.

They don't bother with the trap anymore, and it's lying with its shafts pointing up at the sky. Each day the brass bits that Dadda used to love to see gleaming are growing duller, and in places they have turned green. You can hardly tell that they are brass at all.

I've been going out to the near meadow to see the chestnut mare. She is my favorite of all the Shires. Her coat is the color of honey and of amber, and her mane and tail are paler, like a buff envelope. She has a white blaze tapering down to her velvety nose, and when she sees me, she whickers softly and pricks up her ears as I climb over the gate.

She has her foal with her, and he dances beside her as she walks over to me. His legs are so long that he looks like a sprite dancing on the air. His tail is not like an adult's, but like a soft pad covered in soft hair, and, instead of brushing it from side to side like his mother, he flaps it up and down. The mare is always pleased to see me and enjoys showing off her foal to me. She talks to me about him, nudging him with her nose, and she stands patiently while he butts her with his head to make the milk flow faster when he feeds from her.

I take John with me this morning, because he catches sight of me as I am walking behind the cow house along the path to the meadow. He isn't too bad, though he does insist on trying to touch the foal, which makes the mare nervous because she doesn't know him like she knows me. Of course it would have to be at that moment that Anne appears at the gate, just in time to see the mare put her ears back and roll her eyes at John.

"I'm going to tell Mammy of you," she yells. "Yah! Caught you! You know you're not supposed to go near the horses!"

And off she flies, full of her own importance. Damn her to hell! She won't come into the meadow; it is too muddy and might spoil her shoes. But she is mad at us, because she thinks we're leaving her out of something. So she has to get us in trouble!

John says, "Let's go back, before she comes," but I say, "No, you go back if you want, but I'm staying here." He hangs around me for a minute, unsure of what to do, and then he wanders over to the ditch to scramble around among the bushes, pretending to be busy.

I stay with the mare, soothing her and stroking her strong neck. She keeps her eyes on John until she is sure he isn't going to bother the foal, and then she bends down her head and pushes it into my stomach, nudging me forgivingly. I put my arms around her neck and bury my head in the hard, warm hollow there, breathing in the sharp and powerful scent of her, curling my fingers in the long coarse strands of her mane. I feel so full of love for her and for her foal, and she knows this, and speaks to me from her busy nostrils.

It is so simple, the love I feel for the horses. If I love them they love me back, and there is no confusion between us. There are no words to find, and no embarrassment to swallow. I love their huge bodies moving around me, their heads curving round, and most of all the smell that I can lose myself in, against the touch of their skin.

"Mary! Mary! You cursed child! Will you come out of that field! Come over here, this minute!"

Mammy is over at the gate, waving wildly, with Anne settling down beside her for the fray, perched on the lowest bar. I close my eyes and whisper good-bye to the mare, soaking her smell into me, and she sweeps her head up to watch my mother. The foal dances round me for a few paces and then runs back to his mother as I walk unwillingly across the meadow toward mine.

"Sure God help us, won't you be killed meddling with the foal! How many times do you have to be told to stay away from the horses? If poor Dadda was here, he'd take a strap to you, God forgive me."

I am tired suddenly, tired and utterly wretched. Are my only friends in the whole world really to be barred from me now? Anne stands swinging on the gate, her eyes greedy for a confrontation between me and Mammy. I swallow and take a deep breath, ordering the tears which are stinging my eyes to go back. I don't want to cry. I want to stick up for myself.

"Mammy," I begin quietly, "I wasn't doing any harm. The mare knows me. And if Dadda was still here, he wouldn't mind. You know he wouldn't. He used to say I had a feel for the horses, just like him."

She looks at me and says nothing, but she pulls me roughly as I climb over the gate and gives me a slap as I land on the other side. I'm so sick of her slapping me.

"Mammy, please believe me when I say I do know what I'm doing. I'm not entirely stupid, you know."

I don't raise my voice. Her eyes flicker away as I try to look at them. Why, oh why, won't she let me reach her? She grabs me by the shoulder, grumbling, and brushes at my skirt with a hand that is none too gentle.

"Lookit your good skirt, ruined with the mud. And who's going to wash it, might I ask? Anne, will you get down from there and go and help your granny wash the spuds. Go on, now, and stop your gawping. John! John! Come out of that meadow, now, this instant!"

Anne runs off, singing, determined to be the model child, and I stand miserably waiting for John with Mammy. He is making his way back slowly, poking a stick nonchalantly into the bushes to show he isn't scared and has all the time in the world. The sky is white, and there is no color in the land.

My mother and I stand side by side, but we are so separate from each other that I can hardly believe she is my mother or has ever had anything to do with me at all. She carries on shouting at John to hurry up. I fix my eyes on the one point of color in the world: the bright coat of the mare as she turns and, with a sweep of her tail, canters to the other side of the meadow, with her foal bucking like a little rocking horse beside her.

✑ Twenty

In one of Nuala's magazines, there's an article about a famous film star and her mother. She's my best friend, says the film star. She's more like my sister than my mother.

Mammy and Nuala are in the back kitchen, washing up. They are giggling and falling about as they talk. Their voices rise and fall and go on and on. I'm scared that they might be talking about me. They might be laughing about me! I feel hot with anger. I've never heard Mammy laugh as much as she's been doing here lately, whenever she and Nuala go off together.

Why can't she be like that with me?

Nuala lends me her makeup. I put on some mascara, and Nuala shows me how to draw a fine line with the eyeliner. Then she puts some white lipstick onto my mouth. I look in the mirror. Nuala says, "You have fine eyes and good bone structure." I run off to show Mammy. "Wipe that muck off your eyes," she says. "And what's that on your mouth? You look like a corpse."

But if I really was a corpse, perhaps she'd prefer it. I

wouldn't be able to talk or have any opinions at all, so she'd have nothing to complain of. Sometimes I think she must have taken the wrong baby home at the hospital. But Nuala says, "You have your mammy's eyes, and her fine thick hair."

❧ Twenty-one

Sundays are so difficult. We have to go to Mass. This means an hour of Mammy nagging and criticizing. Anne doesn't mind; she puts on her pink dress with the frills, her white shoes and socks and matching gloves, and then Mammy brushes out her golden hair so it ripples down her back and tops it off with a little straw hat with flowers on the brim. Anne looks sweet; so pink and delicious you could eat her. And she knows it.

But me and John suffer tortures. John gets dressed in his little good-boy suit and a shirt with a collar so stiff he says it feels like a plate round his neck. Then Mammy fixes a tie on him, and her fingers are so nervous that she does it wrong two or three times and slaps the backs of his legs because of course it's all his fault. And then she wets her hairbrush and does his hair, plastering it to his skull with a side parting so straight it looks like a white scar on his head. He stands there, utterly miserable, looking like a miniature bank clerk. Mammy likes this: "You look like a proper little man," she says with satisfaction.

For me it's worst of all. I have to change my clothes

altogether two or three times, because she doesn't like
the short black skirt or the yellow minidress. I end up
wearing one of her suits, with one of her hats. I look ridiculous. I scream at her, "You want me to look ridiculous! I didn't ask to be born! I wish I was dead!"

I stand appalled at what I've said, waiting for her fury
to lash out at me. But her face looks gray suddenly,
drawn and tired, and as she turns her eyes away from
me I see a film of sadness pass over them. And all she
says is "God forgive you," in a quiet, drained tone of
voice, so I know that I have wounded her. I can't bear
it when she goes quiet like this.

The journey to the church, with her still sitting so
tired and silent next to me, is torture. I'm almost glad
when I feel her eyes on us again as we walk up the pathway to the church. She's rallied herself once more, ready
to attack if we put a foot wrong.

In the church Daddy and John sit on one side, with
the men, and we sit on the other, with the women.
Mammy pinches me as I sit down, pointing at my knees.
I cover them and don't dare answer her back, because
Granny and Nuala are here too. Nuala has on a little
red pillbox hat. Granny kneels over her rosary beads
with her lips moving. Feet shuffle on the bare boards.
When everyone lowers their heads, I keep mine upright. All around me there are bowed heads and fingers
moving over rosary beads. I feel so bored and stifled.
My jaws ache from swallowing yawns.

After Mass, we all amble out into the churchyard.

The men stand in clusters against the walls, lighting up cigarettes. People gather around us, greeting Mammy, bowing before Granny. Mammy pulls us forward and people look us up and down and cluck over us, prodding us as though we are turkeys being fattened up. Mammy stands with her face red as people admire Anne's curls and John's little suit. She says, "Mary came top of her class this last term." People look at me. "Thanks be to God," they say.

I stand with Granny at Dadda's headstone. She holds my hand as she lowers herself slowly to her knees. I watch her as she bows her head and prays, her whisper louder than the voices round us, it seems to me. I think of Dadda, moldering under the ground where I stand.

I run down the path to the gates and stand by the hedge, looking over the field behind the creamery. I used to come here with him every morning. I let the tears fall from my eyes, warm wet tears pouring down my face.

As I stand there sobbing, I feel a pinch on my arm so hard it makes me gasp. Mammy is saying, "Sure God in heaven, why must you always be disgracing me so? Running away from poor Dadda's grave, and all those old yokes looking at you. Why can't you say your prayers, like a normal person?"

Her face is distraught. I've let her down again. Everything I do is wrong.

✖ Twenty-two

"There's no better day than today, sure," Granny is saying. "We'll do it today, allanah."

My heart is low. I'm trying to be Granny's willing helper, but I feel so low. And her words make me feel lower still. I know that she's talking about clearing out the sow house. She's been saying how it's in a dreadful state, what with the eleven babies all pissing and shitting in there, as well as their mother. The hen- and calf houses have a dry, aromatic warmth to them, but the sow house really stinks, and it is running with rank liquids. My heart is heavy as I follow her around feeding the animals and collecting eggs. I'm dreading what's coming next.

"Sure pigs is the cleanest animals on God's earth," Granny is saying as we tramp across the yard to the sow-house door, bearing our broom and shovel. "They do hate to be living in filth and desolation." As we stand by the closed door, I try hard not to think that the smells coming out are the stink of danger.

Dadda never used to deal with the sows when once they'd had their babies. He always stood back before my granny when faced with a savage and protective she-pig with her young. His father before him had lost the use of a leg, shattered the length of its shin, because of a sow. A sow whose jaws are as long as a man's arm from fingertip to elbow. I shiver now as I remember how he used to tell us this, to stop us from going near the sow house.

But here I am now, standing at the door, about to go in. I think to myself, my legs will be a great source of interest to those little piglets. I can hear their excited squealings and snufflings behind the door. And maybe their mother will want to tear them bloody from their sockets, these legs of mine.

"We'll back the old one into the far corner, by the window," Granny is saying, "and then like a good girl you'll go over the floor with the yard broom while I feed her." My spirits sink even lower. The bonhams will rush to the interesting swoosh and scrape of the broom, like iron filings to a magnet, and what will the sow do then? And what will I do? And what on earth will Granny be able to do, for all her grand touch with the sows?

Miserably I stand beside her as she undoes the latch. The sharp and bitter smell seeps out at us. She is pausing for a second with her hand on the latch, and she seems to have started to breathe in a new way. And it can't be because of the smell, because her lips are moving in the same way that they do at Mass, when she silently says her prayers. It seems to me too that her little body has become more strong looking, more compact and gathered together for action.

She begins a low, soft croon, whose words, if words they are, are not comprehensible to me. Holding her pail of food at arm's length, she opens the door. I know that she wants me to follow behind the pail, and that she is using it to shield me. I grasp the wooden handle of the broom and follow close behind her, trying to hold my breath against the smell.

It is dark in the sow house, and my feet are slithering on the liquefying floor. I feel fear shooting down into my knickers, in a sharp point between my legs. I realize that my eyes are shut, so I open them. Punched in the stomach by the smell, I move forward behind her, hearing the scampering feet of the piglets skittering across the floor. Their little noses, like flat round pennies, are twitching and nudging at my feet.

They are so sweet, baby pigs, but the deep warning growl of their mother sends fear trickling down my back again. I stand still while Granny edges forward, crooning and lowing. The great bulk in the center of the house moves, and as the pale light from a tiny slit in the wall touches her back I see her head swaying and weaving to the sounds that Granny is making. Clucking and crowing, Granny empties the food into the trough, her eyes never leaving the sow.

"Set to now, Mary," she whispers as the piglets scatter to the sounds and smells issuing from the trough. I edge to the back of the building and start to push the broom head through the thick liquid, shoving it toward the door. Still crooning, Granny is stirring the mash around in the trough with her hand, and the growls of the sow seem to become louder and more full of protest. "Ah, whisht," says Granny to her. "Get away wit' you," she adds, almost as though she's teasing.

She bends sturdily over the trough, muttering and grousing. The sow looks up at her, flapping her huge ears as food dribbles from her jaws, her small wicked eyes gleaming. The sow is grunting and Granny is scolding; the sow complains and Granny grumbles. For a moment they sound like a pair of very old women, gossiping in the corner, complaining and chivvying.

I wonder, does the sow remember how Granny helped her at her farrowing? Granny is resting her hand on the huge back, scratching the tough skin, and the sow has a faraway look in her uplifted eyes. "Ah well," sighs Granny, "are we not one and the same, you and I, poor owld soul? Are we not one and the same altogether, allanah? Whisht now, so." She lowers herself to her knees, and I am astonished at the sight of my respectable granny, sitting back on her heels, chatting away companionably with the vast, dirt-smeared, pendulous bulk of the animal who is gulping and slurping, belching and grunting next to her.

I am shocked. I have never seen Granny like this before. In confusion, I run out to grab the shovel from against the wall, and then I go back in to heave dripping spadefuls out into the yard as fast as I can. Granny continues her crooning, as though she is sharing something with this animal! Not until I've almost finished does she get up and join me, wiping her hands on her overalls.

"Ah well, is it not a job well done, Mary," she approves. "Come away now, and we'll get some good straw to throw in with her, a fine thick dry bed for her to rest her poor bones upon."

❧ Twenty-three

Another long, empty afternoon is looming when once more Nuala comes to my rescue. "Come and help me with the laundry, will you, Mary," she says, so I go out with her to the haggard to fold the dry sheets.

I'm glad of something to do, and glad that I've got her to myself for a while. There is something about folding sheets that is pleasant and peaceful. You have to be feeling all right with the person you're doing it with or the sheets end up all wrong, lumpy and twisted, with bits hanging down in all the wrong places. Anne and I have had terrible fights over it in the past.

You have to take the sheet by two corners, shake it between you so that it billows open, fold it cleanly in half, shake it again to snap the fold into place, and then walk to meet each other, to fold it in half that way. Then you grab the bottom edge and do the same again, half, then half again. It's satisfying to make each sheet neat and folded, and to build up a crisp pile from the tumbled heaps you've piled up from the bushes.

Nuala and I work pleasantly, in silence, shaking the sheets and stepping up to each other, almost like a stately and rhythmic dance. As we meet in the middle with our arms outstretched, holding up the corners, our faces smile at each other. I'm plucking up courage to talk with her again, to follow on from where we left off in the car, when suddenly she sighs and breaks the silence.

"Well, Mary, I'm at a loss what to do, so I am."

I'm startled; merry Nuala, at a loss? "I don't know what you mean, Nuala," I reply.

She smiles and shakes her head. "Ah well," she laughs, "sure of course you don't! Wait till I tell you. What is foxing me till I'm near killed thinking about it is this. Should I go back to the U.S. of A., and get a job, and settle there, or should I just carry on here with your granny?" She is gazing at me frankly, and her face is serious now. "You see, if I stayed here, could I stand it? I'd have no job, sure, and never a hope of getting one. I'd have to stay here around the house, and wait for the day some fine prince would come and take me away to marry him!"

Her eyes are laughing again, above the sadness, and I grin back at her. I can't imagine Nuala just hanging around, somehow! As we snap a fold into place, I suddenly realize that she is really asking me for my opinion! This makes me feel privileged, but then I feel very ignorant as I realize that I don't know what to say to her. So I ask her a question instead.

"What's it like in New York?"

"Ah well, sure." Her face is lowered as she places the

sheet on the pile and stoops to pick up another one from the heap. "It's a huge teeming place, buildings and filth as far as the eye can see. It can be great if you're young and fit and if you've plenty of money to see you through. There's a song that says the streets are paved with gold over there." She laughs with bitterness. "But what I saw on the streets was a different story. People lying down and dying because there's nowhere else for them to go. Lying out there on the sidewalks, under bits of cardboard."

Holding a sheet against herself, she is looking through me, into the distance of her own thoughts. She sighs. "But sure, the odd thing is, you just get used to it after a while. The main thing, as far as I'm concerned, is that I could easily get a job there. Plus, the people there are more free and easy in their ways. I'd have no yokes looking at my red hat over there, like they did here after Mass on Sunday!"

She laughs again, but with more merriment this time. I'm looking at her in surprise. "Oh yes, Mary," she giggles, "they do all be going on at me here about my clothes—my skirts are scandalous short, hadn't you noticed?—and my smoking, and they think I'm a terrible shreel to be going off down to Kilkenny at night on me own for a bit of a dance! That's it, you see, Mary. There isn't much of what you'd call freedom here, for the likes of me."

I'm so excited suddenly. She's talking about some of the exact same things that have been bothering me about being here! All that business about knees, and clothes, and what you should and shouldn't do, and going to Mass! I listen to her eagerly.

"But there again, Mary, if I was to go back there and get a job, and clear the cockroaches out of me cupboards, and settle down again nice and easy, wouldn't I feel awful lonely sometimes. It's not me home, d'you see? I wouldn't have much in the way of company around me. I'd have to make a place for meself there, whereas here, it's all laid out for me. And if I did decide to get married there, how would I be fixed, bringing up me kids as Yankees? Sure, they'd have American accents and wouldn't even talk the same as me!"

"Yes, Nuala," I say eagerly. "I know what you mean! It's like that for me. In England, Mammy says people make fun of her for talking Irish, you know. And I get embarrassed about her on speech day at school if my friends hear her. But here, it's me that feels all wrong. My voice sounds all wrong here compared to everyone else's."

She's listening to me reflectively, and then she shakes the sheet toward me, and we begin to fold it up together. "I knew you'd have something to say on the matter," she says after a little while. "That time we were in the car . . . you were telling me some things . . ."

Suddenly I'm talking to her in a rush. "Yes . . . you said to me that all I have to do is be strong and everything will be all right, that's what you said. But Nuala, it's not as easy as you think. The girls at school make fun of me for being Irish ... those stupid jokes, you know, being thick and stuff. And Mammy makes it worse ... *she* never goes out or talks to anyone—except at the church—and she expects me to do the same."

Nuala takes the sheet from me as I walk through the final folds, and as she stoops for another one I carry on, remembering the loneliness, the feeling of being trapped. "The girls all think I'm weird for being Irish, but if I could get to know them, it might be different. But Mammy never *ever* lets me go out with them, at weekends and stuff, so I never have a chance to get to know them. And so they think I'm even weirder, because I never go out with them. Weird or a snob. They talk to each other about what they did at the weekends ... or what they're going to do ... and I have nothing to say ..."

My face goes red as I find myself saying, "... nothing to say, unless I make it up ..." "Telling lies?" Nuala is surprised. "Yes, about things I did at the weekend ..." "And aren't you afraid of getting caught out?" she asks. Panic chases up my back as I whisper, "Oh God yes, Nuala, I am."

Holding the bundled sheet in her arms, Nuala's face is sad when I raise my eyes to hers. "So you see, Nuala, if I was strong, like you say, what difference would it make? I'd still be lonely, nothing would have changed. What's the point in being 'strong' when you've got no friends?"

"Mary, allanah," she says quietly, "your mammy is

awful lonely too." I turn from her impatiently, but her voice is firm. "No, listen to me," she says. "Listen till I tell you about your mammy." She sighs and looks out past me, over the haggard to the trees beyond. "All on her own, your mammy went to England, and she knew no one, and then she met your daddy and they settled down, but they still knew no one. And soon she was alone in the house with her kids to bring up. So, she looked forward all the year long to coming back here and having everyone make her feel at home, and having a gas in the evenings with the rest of us round the fire.

"But when she was back here, all the old ones were watching her, and watching you kids, to see was she bringing you up right over there in heathen England. Sure, she hasn't an idea how English people bring up their kids, and she's afraid that the people here will think she's brought you up mannerless and heathen. So she has only the example of Dadda, how he brought us up. And Dadda had no light hand with the switch, let me tell you."

I'm struggling to understand what she's saying, to look at Mammy in the way she's asking me to. But all I can think of are the bamboo sticks that Mammy lets Daddy hit us with at home and the hours of loneliness and boredom there. "But Nuala," I protest, "I'm not you, and my daddy isn't Dadda, and where we live, it's totally different to here. And *I* have to live there."

"Mary, allanah, try not to be too hard on your mammy," she says, and I raise my eyes to the heavens.

But Nuala's voice comes back at me with more force. "Mary, don't you see that I'm listening to you? Don't you see that I'm taking in your every word? Sure, if I had Yankee children, wouldn't I be in the same fix your mammy's in, trying to bring them up between two worlds? And wouldn't my heart be grieving for them too, like it's grieving for you right now? But how can I stay here? Sure Jaysus, I'm killed thinking about it!"

Her knuckles whiten as she clenches her fists against the sheet she's holding. And then she starts to shake it loose, flapping it with a crack on the air. "Listen, Mary," she says, with her face sober. "I'll try and help you. I'll have a word with your mammy. No, no, don't worry, I won't let on that you've spoken to me. I'll just ask her advice about me own dilemma and see how we go from there. She knows how hard it is bringing up your kids in a country where you're a foreigner, and a despised one at that. It's a tragic state this country's in, with all the young people leaving it and all the ones that rule it doing nothing but tucking themselves into England's pockets."

She waves the sheet at me, and her voice has a bitterness I've never heard before. Then she raises her eyes to mine and says, "There. That's what I'll try to do for you. But I'm wanting you to do something for me as well now, mind."

Surprised, I scan her face. Do something for Nuala? How can I do that? What way can I possibly be of use to her? But of course I'll try. I'll do anything she asks me to if I can. I'm anxious as I think I might let her down. "Yes, Nuala ... of course I will ... but what is it?"

Her eyes are glued to mine as she speaks to me then. "Mary, I'd like you to try and think of my imaginary Yankee children. Think of what I could say to them if they showed signs of rejecting me ... of being miserable in the country I'd brought them into. You know the score sure, I know you do. So, could you put your mind to that for me when you've a spare moment, like, allanah?"

✿ Twenty-four

I have something else to think of now. I have to think of this problem of Nuala's. I shuffle it about in my mind, wondering what I could say to her. And also, I have a small bright hope that she has given me. I feel sure that she'll be able to talk to Mammy and explain things to her so that Mammy will understand. I wait patiently for the moment when she'll come and talk to me again, after her chat with Mammy.

But then suddenly, out of the blue, everything starts to fall apart. I find Anne reading my sketchbook. She has found it where I hid it, behind the big wardrobe. And suddenly my temper explodes, and I'm quarreling with her and everything is out of control. She runs off with my book. She says she's going to show it to Daddy! I'm nearly crying. Why can't my sister be my friend? Why are my parents my enemies?

She is running down the stairs with me chasing after her. So steep they are, the stairs, I'm afraid she'll fall, and then I'll be in even more trouble. John is coming in from the yard and he bumps straight into her as she reaches the bottom of the stairs. "Get off!" she shouts, grabbing the book to her chest, but he's sensed a bit of fun. He snatches it from her and runs right out the door.

I run after him, feeling calmer, calling, "John! Come back! It's mine, not Anne's!" He's usually quite a good little friend of mine, but this time the devil must be in him. He giggles at me over his shoulder and runs off round the side of the house, toward the haggard. I'm blind with panic, drowning in fear. I grab a pitchfork from against the wall and chase after him, waving the fork at him. "Come back! Come back or I'll kill you when I catch you!" But he's having great sport, watching me chase him and dodging round the other side of the house.

"Ha, ha! I've got you now," I mutter, and I double back and run through the gap between the house and the cart house, where the vehicles are stored. But the concrete under my feet is wet and slimy from the water that comes from the waste pipe of the sink in the back kitchen, and as I run the legs fly out from under me and I slither forward. I'm flailing to get my balance just as he belts round the corner right into me. And in one awful second I feel the wildly waving point of the pitchfork sink in through his Wellington and into his foot.

He is lying on the ground, appalled and white as a sheet. My head is blind with shock—and then he starts screaming. I yank the pitchfork out of his foot. I feel like a monster. I see my sketchbook lying forgotten in the filthy black sludge. I grab it, hissing at him, "Serves you right, you little tyke. I told you I'd kill you!" Then I run, as fast as I can, to the hay barn.

I clamber up to my sanctuary and reach the top just as Mammy, Nuala, and Granny all come running from different directions. They drag John out of the narrow passageway. He is wailing and screaming. "She tried to kill me, Mammy! Mary said she was going to kill me!" Oh, Nuala! What must Nuala think of me! Mammy is shrieking and yelling, "Sure God help us, what is the matter with that shreel of a girl that she does want to be killing her little brother? Oh God, lookit the innocent soul of him, as white as the angels!" And now Anne is sidling up, putting her oar in. "She's got a screw loose, if you ask me, Mammy. She was after me too." Everything is shattered. There are splinters in my eyes.

Mammy is standing up now, wild with distraction but purposeful with her orders. "Nuala, go you in the Ford Popular and get Doctor O'Connell here. Hurry yourself now, before the septicemia sets in, God help us!" Nuala runs off, and Mammy and Granny carry John into the house.

My mouth is dry. I'm clutching my sketchbook to my heart. I can't stop shaking. Oh God, what have I done? It seems like hours before the doctor's big Rover comes nosing into the yard, with the dogs leaping round it trying to take mouthfuls out of the tires. Mammy comes flying out of the house, greeting the doctor as though he's God himself. They disappear into the house. My teeth are chattering, although it isn't cold.

Twenty-five

I'm frozen with shock. I can hardly move, but I've got to find out what I've done to John. I decide I've got to creep into the house to find out what I can without being seen. They'll all be in the big bedroom upstairs. So I slither down the hay, my stomach pummeling my throat, and run toward the house. My legs feel like empty sticks, so weak it's hard to get them to move. But I get to the house door somehow, and then I creep up the stairs like a silent, desperate ghost, avoiding all the places where the boards creak. I stand on the landing, out of sight beside the open door.

The doctor's voice is comfortable. "Sure, what possessed your sister to do that to you anyway?" Anne pipes up with her sneaky whine. "She's got a book that she writes things in, and it's all about us, and I found it, and it's got rude bits in it about Mammy and Daddy, and I found it and she chased me because I wouldn't give it back, and so I gave it to John and he ran off with it, and she said she was going to kill him, and now he's got blood poisoning."

John opens his lungs and wails. Mammy seems to be

shaking Anne. "Sure will you hold your tongue and don't be making things worse than they are! God help me, Doctor, am I not near killed with these eejits of kids. Leave your brother alone. Hasn't he had a grand injection now! Ah John, will you whisht your noise!" John starts hiccuping wetly. "Have I got blood poisoning, Doctor?" "Well, young man, it's a puncture wound, and it's very dirty, but I don't think you'll be losing your leg."

Losing his leg! Oh God, I didn't mean it. The doctor's nice Dublin voice is punishing me. "So, you'll be leathering the daughter for this now, won't you, Bridie?" he is saying conversationally. "Oh sure, by the howneyman, she'll have the biggest hiding of her life after this when we find her." There is no room for doubt in Mammy's voice.

My heart sinks down to my belly. There is nothing left for me here now. I'll fly away, away from the whole bloody lot of them.

I'm down the stairs and out the door and off out into the haggard as fast as I can go. My legs are strong with a sense of purpose now. I run through the bushes to the fence that leads to the far meadow, and then I'm off. I can't wait to leave it all behind. The blood is pumping in my head like a piston. My legs are hurling the field away behind me.

But suddenly the sounds of my feet, of my panting breath, of the thudding blood in my temples seem to have become amplified. The ground is thudding louder than my head. I turn around, and horror lurches in my belly. A whole field full of young bullocks is coming after me! They must have been clustered out of sight behind the trees as I came flying through the fence.

Oh God, I'm scared! Their heads are low and shaking from side to side, and their ponderous bodies are massing together as they buck with their back legs. I turn and drag my legs through the tussocky grass toward the gate on the other side. It is like one of those nightmares where you are running away from something but your legs are being pulled down like heavy lead, and you're hauling them through liquid cement. The meadow is long, so long, and I'm running at full tilt and the gate is so far away!

I'm exhausted by the time I reach it. My breath is hacking through my lungs and my thighs are trembling. I know I'll never be able to get them to heave my body over the gate! I wrench at the hasp instead to unlatch the gate, and it swings open easily on its well-hung hinges. Oh God, too easily, for as I foolishly take my hand from it, it lazily swings wide open. I'm through to the lane, but I can only watch in horror as the gate sways away from me. I know I do not dare to run after it before the bullocks reach it. They are bunching together now, all heading for the same opening like one huge, lumbering mass, and I throw myself onto the ditch as they all come tumbling through, out into the lane.

Once they are in the lane, they slow down, shaking

their heads and rolling their eyes, staggering up onto each other's backs with their forelegs, flicking their tails as they realize they are in a strange place. I lie on the bank, my ears thumping. I will be in such trouble now as doesn't even bear thinking about! Somehow I *have* to catch them.

I raise myself to my feet and start to move toward them. And of course, when they sense me behind them, they turn and trot away from me down the lane. What a fool I am! Oh God, what *am* I to do? The only thing I can think of doing is to stay with them as they move down the lane. So I walk along behind them, and the more I walk, the more they walk too. It's only then that I start to cry, as I see their tails flicking at me while they shamble inexorably on ahead of me. I really don't know what to do to get them to turn back up the lane toward the meadow again. The only thing I can think of to comfort myself with is the fact that they are going *up* the lane away from the house, and no one will see them.

I carry on, sniveling and clutching my sketchbook, for what seems like hours. Sometimes they pause to snatch at mouthfuls of the thick grass and flowers on the ditches, and I think, If only I can edge past them now and turn them round! But their big liquid eyes are too quick for me, and each time I try to slip by them, they kick up their heels and scurry on.

I am worn out with tears and worry by the time I notice that it's getting colder, and that dusk is draining all the color from the land. I stop and stand in the middle of the lane. It is almost as though the dusk is draining all the life from me too as I watch them ambling on ahead of me into the gathering shadows. There is nothing more that I can do. I am exhausted and my eyes feel raw and bloodshot.

But as I stand there, probing the distance with my bleary eyes, I slowly realize that they are coming to a halt. Of course! Now that I've stood perfectly still, they are settling down too. I feel an utter fool as I watch them graze in the twilight, in the long grasses waving at the side of the lane. I should have done this ages ago! They seem quite content, their long tongues curling around the timothy grass, savoring the new flavors.

I walk over to the ditch and sit down. The sky is turning dark. It is royal blue and streaked like shot silk. To my right it is dappled with blazing light. I watch the trails of cloud slowly change color, shifting from gold to amber, from pink to deep red. I've never sat and watched the sunset before. And it is so beautiful that it takes my breath away.

The sun is hanging, spinning in the branches of a tree, and its scarlet light seems to bathe my eyes with liquid. It turns the branches of the tree to black, and the bushes too, etching their contours against the sky. The sky is vast, radiant with colors splashing across the four horizons. It feels as though an orchestra is playing in color, blazing in the sky.

And then the ball of the sun hangs poised for a second before dropping, like a gigantic sweet, below the horizon. The dark shapes of the cattle rustling near me seem to have lost their threat, and everything is bathed in gentleness. It will all be all right in the end, I say to myself, and I keep hold of that thought, though I do not have a clue what to do next. I am beginning to feel cold, and a damp mist seems to be rising from the gray fields and from the bank on which I'm sitting. But I don't dare move as I keep softly whispering, "It will all be all right in the end."

Suddenly I hear the cattle shifting, and I can see the whites of their eyes rolling as they strain their ears after the faint sound which is plucking the distance. It is a regular squeak, metal against metal, and a slow and steady creaking sound. I look up. A bicycle! And yes, I can see the thin beam of light from its lamp, wobbling among the branches of the hedges. My faith has worked!

I don't dare move as the cattle start to fidget and slowly shift along back in my direction. A man's voice is saying softly, "Sure what are these lads doing, wandering freely along the highway? Come up now lads, till we see." The light from his lamp is stationary now; he has dismounted. The cattle are all bunching together, moving slowly past me where I am sitting quietly. When the bicycle light draws level with me, I stand up, feeling relieved and embarrassed.

"Hello there," I call softly. He peers through the dusk at me. "God's truth," he says, making the sign of the cross, "did I not think that you were the banshee, rising up at me from out of the dark mists!" "I'm real," I stammer as he stares at me. His eyes suddenly have a wise air about them. "Sure God, aren't these Michael Kelly's cattle, God rest his soul?" "They are," say I, "and I'm grateful to you for coming along just now. I stupidly let them out of the far meadow and have no idea how to get them back." He peers at me closely and says, "Is it Bridie Kelly's child y'are?" "Yes," say I. "I'm staying with my granny." "Well, I'll be bet," he chuckles, "and you'll be in for a belting now, of that I can be sure!" My heart thumps, but he is taking pity on me. "I'll tell you what we'll do," he murmurs confidingly. "We'll drive them home and get them in at the gate, and no one'll be any the wiser! What do you say to that?"

Well of course, I'm not arguing with that. So we walk along the dark lanes together, in the silence and secrecy of the peaceful dusk. Already my heart is lighter. When we draw near to the gateway, he drops his bicycle onto the ground and skirts round up onto the ditch, keeping low, to overtake the cattle. They are suspicious, but he is so quick that he easily blocks the lane beyond the gateway into the meadow, and in they cluster. And he closes the gate after them.

It is as simple as that! The nightmare is over. We both lean over the gate, watching them spread out and disappear into the enfolding shadows, and he chuckles again, a soft low sound. "Well, they'll have had fine sport, with their little adventure!" I laugh too, now that it's all over. "Thank you very much for helping me," I say. "Sure, it was nothing," he replies. "I'm glad to have been in the right place at the right time, for a wonder."

He mounts his bicycle and continues on his way, with a friendly wave and a "Good luck to you now!" The dogs suddenly start barking wildly up ahead. They can hear him coming. I hear muffled voices, and then silence. I am hungry and cold, but I do not want to go back to face my punishment. I think I'll hide in the stable, in the warmth with the horses, and then I can slip away in the morning before anyone gets up. I wonder how John is ... poor John ...

And now suddenly here is Prince, leaping and grinning up to me, his tail waving hazily through the dusk. I hear running feet in the distance. Oh, Prince, you have given me away! Something makes me scramble up the ditch and hide my sketchbook, tucked well in behind the bushes at the top. It will get damp, but at least it will be safe from prying eyes.

I jump down just as Billy comes running up. It's time to face the music now, for sure.

🌿 Twenty-six

Never has the warm light flooding from the windows of the house seemed so threatening. We walk through the yard, and even the lolloping dogs cannot ease my fear. Billy opens the house door to let me in, but he stays outside, closing it just as my parents both turn their heads round to look at me. They stand up, and their faces lunge at me and their words whip me as they walk toward me. I stand against the wall, and my head bounces back from it with the rebound of my father's first blow.

I am stunned. I can see stars, I really can, and through the spinning of lights I hear their voices chanting out a catalogue of my wickedness.

"You nearly killed your brother! Sure God's truth what'll we do with you?"

"Shaming us in front of your granny! Have you no remorse in your wicked soul!"

"And what about this filthy book you're writing in, eh? Eh? ..." Daddy's fist hits my head again. I must look as ill as I feel, because Mammy is screaming at him, "Not her head! Mind her head! Here, use this!" I see her giving him a long, slim switch, like the ones they use for bringing in the cows. Then he hits me everywhere he can reach as I try to shield myself with my hands and arms. I can feel the stinging lashes on my arms, my legs, my back.

"I'm sorry!" I scream, but he won't stop until eventually Granny comes running from the back kitchen. Her voice is low and urgent. "Liam! Liam! Stop it now! Sure that's enough." I glimpse Anne in the doorway behind her; her eyes are cruel and greedy slits. Daddy is roaring and red in the face, and Mammy pulls back his arm as he raises it for another stream of blows. I can hear him panting. I stand with my head thudding and my body screaming. I can't remember what it is I'm being punished for. All I can feel is pain, pain and bright fury.

They all move away from me and mill around the kitchen. The lamplight makes it all seem unreal to me, like a film. Mammy is almost crying. "Sure, why can't you behave? You'll give your father a heart attack, so you will!" Granny has taken the switch from my father, who is ashen as he wipes his sweating forehead, and she slips it in among the sticks of wood at the side of the fire. Daddy doesn't look at me as he says, "Go to bed now, and say a prayer for your sins."

I sniff the snot up into my nose and swallow. Sins? What sins? I force my voice not to quaver as I say, "I've committed no sins! It was all an accident. I did not mean to do any of it." Daddy lunges at me again with his fist up, but Mammy grabs him, shielding me from him, screaming, "For God's sake will you get out of here! Go up to bed this minute, can't you!"

I turn and go out the door and up the stairs. From nothing, everything has exploded into a nightmare. I remember the chuckles of the man who helped me, and I wonder why my father can't make light of things like he did. I crawl into bed fully clothed and carefully hold my body. John is breathing quietly and steadily across the room, sleeping peacefully. He must be all right then, at least.

I'm so bruised, so battered, so ashamed. I'm so glad Nuala wasn't there to see it. I must be really bad for Daddy to have done this to me. But can I really be as wicked as these welts on my arms, as this buzzing in my head? My face is sticky with tears and snot and my hands feel grimy and swollen.

I'm hot, but I'm shivering as I stare through the darkness at the familiar shapes of the furniture and at the pale rectangle of the window. At the far side of the room, where the mantelpiece is, I see the pale blue translucent light of the statue hovering in the shadows. How lovely it would be to be like that, without a body to hurt me, to be nothing but a clear light. I find myself whispering, "Tower of ivory, mystical rose, can you help me?"

✍ Twenty-seven

In the hay barn, high up, hiding, hiding.

My sketchbook was smeared with damp when I found it and the pages were soft, but it is safe, at least. I hide it up here, in a hollow in the hay, or between two mossy stones in the back wall of the stables. The horses and the hay can be its guardians.

Under threat. I feel under threat. People's faces are like masks. Their skin stretches into slits across their teeth when they talk to me, and their voices come from far away. I do not speak. My fingers are like dough, numb and dumb. Hanging from my arms, all thumbs. I avoid Nuala. I would be ashamed if her eyes met mine.

I creep up into the bedroom to see John. He smiles and says, "I'm sorry, Mary." I want to hug him, to feel his little-boy skin that smells faintly of tin, under my cheek. But my body is swollen and lumbering. "That's all right" is all I say. And I'm sorry too.

In bed all day, he is resting his foot. The prong of the fork went through the narrow bit of flesh between the knob of his ankle bone and the skinny bone at the back of his heel. My stomach clenches. "I'm so sorry, John."

He pulls down the blanket proudly to show me his bandage. "It's all right," he says. "The doctor said it missed the Achilles tendon by a whisker!" I sit and tell him a story. Give him some of my paper to draw on. "Draw me a horse," he says. We are tucked up together in his little bed. Anne comes in. "Go away," he says. "We're busy."

Anne is not to be trusted. I've never spent much time with her, but now I spend none at all. She is greedy for something. She is clutching at something. She is dangerous. Clinging to Daddy, neat and clean. Her eyes dart and swerve, trying to snatch. I hide from her. At night, in bed, her sharp feet kick me if I brush against her in my sleep. I run from the sheets in the morning before she is awake.

Before anyone is awake, I see the sun leaping in the windows. A great silent gaze of light outside. I run from the house, before the people capture it, and I breakfast alone outside on great gusts of air, which fill my lungs. My toes curl in the dew. Dappled, shifting leaves whisper to me; blades of new grass, clear and fine, each one distinct in the sunlight, fill my heart with hope. Birdsong darts and ripples in the air. Frail trails of mist ebb from the valley.

I can live outside, alone. I dig myself small holes to shit in, wipe myself with dock leaves and then bury it. Wash myself with icy water from the well. The bogeyman would be my friend. It takes my breath away and my skin tingles. Then up, up into the hay barn. Sometimes Prince or Molly comes scrambling up behind me, grinning and giggling. They rustle about for rats, talking to me with their eloquent tails. They stretch and yawn, arching their backs as their jaws click, weaving their heads above their outstretched front legs. They doze up here with me, warm bodies to hold, so grateful if I stroke them. And they warn me if someone comes too close.

The fields spread out below us are of forty shades of green. Colors that only happen here, in the Irish light. Mammy used to sing that song to us when we were little. It used to make her cry. When the clouds move over the fields, there are forty more, but darker. When I was little, the bright colors were all I saw. Now I see the clouds pass over, and the colors darken.

Mammy drapes sheets and shirts over the bushes in the haggard down below. The fir trees warn me. She is treacherous. I wanted to be close to her. But she handed Daddy the switch. The hay is being used up in the hay barn. There's not much left. Molly growls, and the fir trees have turned black.

✥ Twenty-eight

John says, "I want to go downstairs." He is fretful in the warm sun pouring in the window. He says his bandage is itching, and he keeps trying to pull it off. "Ah don't, John," I say, but his fingers are scrabbling like crabs. "It's all your fault," he grizzles. I know, I know.

"John, put on your jumper and I'll help you down the stairs! I'll put a chair outside the front door and you can sit there in the sun for a while."

I run downstairs. Good! There is no one about. I get one of the little chairs from beside the fire and I put it outside the door. Then back upstairs. John is sitting good as gold in his jumper. His arm across my shoulder we hop, hop, hop across the bedroom floor, and then slowly down the stairs. He uses his other arm against the wall and levers his way down the steps. Along the hallway and then out, out into the sunshine.

I lower him onto the chair, and then I squat on the concrete beside him. Molly and Prince come weaving up, greedy for strokings. John casts his eyes across the yard, over toward the animal houses on the other side of the wall. There's a commotion coming from the chicken houses. Perhaps someone's laid an egg. It sounds different, though. John is drowsy, with Prince's head, eyes rolling in adoration, resting on his knee. "I wish we had a dog, Mary, you know, at home."

Someone's coming. I can see the top of a head above the yard wall. It's Granny; she won't mind. She is walking toward us now, in full view. She's dangling from one hand two chickens, held upside down by their feet. Their wings are beating like huge fans, scraping her overall. "Two grand birds for tomorrow's dinner," she says with satisfaction. "Mary, hold this one for me, will you?"

She passes me one of the birds, which is struggling and writhing as I take it by its scaly yellow feet. She takes a knife from the top of the yard wall and rubs the blade across the stones to sharpen it. The metal flashes in the sunlight. "Well, John," she smiles, "are you not having a grand time, out in the sunshine at last." And she puts the chicken on the ground, braces its body with her foot, grabs its neck, and slices its head off.

Blood spurts out over the beak and splashes onto the eyes, which are pulsating darkly in surprise. She lets go of it and reaches toward me for the other one, and the headless thing on the ground starts to pump its legs in a mad parody of a gallop as blood continues to pour from the raw neck.

John is crying, gripping the chair. "No, no, don't kill the other one! Why is it doing that if it has no head?" He is trying to back away into the wall, clinging to the chair. I run to him as Granny slices the head off the second one, and I put my arm around him.

"They feel nothing, sure," Granny is saying pleasantly. "It's only the old nerves that do be twitching." She's tied some twine round the feet of one of them, and she's hanging it high on the cart-house wall, out of reach of the dogs. Molly and Prince are trembling beside us. She does the same with the second one, and then she throws the heads to the dogs, who crunch them delightedly between their jaws. Is that what she did with those two dead baby pigs? She wipes the knife on her overalls, back and forth, and replaces it on top of the wall.

The two chickens hang there, their wings twitching feebly, splayed out against the whitewash. The blood is trickling down from their necks, scarlet and glistening. It runs down the wall, which is stained brown from many other deaths, and collects in two pools on the ground. The dogs trot over and lap delicately. The chickens look like upside-down crucifixions.

John's hand on my arm is like a vise. His eyes are dark with shock. "I'm never going to eat roast chicken again," he chokes. He is crying in racking sobs which hurt my heart.

✧ Twenty-nine

The screams are terrible. They are filling my dream. Someone is in agony. Have they dropped the bomb at last?

I am fighting and flailing to drag myself up into consciousness. I want to be awake. I want to be in the real world. I want this nightmare to be over. Huge tides are pulling me down, tugging at my legs. I am being dragged into the fiery pits of hell. The screams of people whose skin and flesh is burning are tearing at my brain. Fever is sweeping through the ship like fire. I claw at the driftwood bobbing in the water near me, and I thrash myself awake. The sheets are choking me, and I struggle onto my elbows to get my head free of them.

I sit up. My head is burning and my hair is glued to my forehead. I am gasping, choking for breath, longing for relief to come flooding back into me, for the familiar shadows of the dark bedroom to settle into place around me.

But something is wrong. The pale rectangle of the window is the wrong color. It is lit up by an eerie, pallid glow. And the screaming—the screaming hasn't stopped! My skin begins to prickle with fear. Oh God, it's not a dream. Mammy! I curl my legs out of the sheets and run to my parents' bed. It is empty. I run to John's. He is lying there, peacefully sleeping. Anne likewise at the end of ours.

Shivering, I run to the window, and I poke my head between the curtains. Half of the yard seems to be on fire! A sheet of blazing heat is roaring among the rooftops to my left, where the chicken house and sow house are. Sparks are rising up in sprays, spitting fire into the air and spiraling back down in slow motion onto the ground. I can see the black ridges of the roof timbers silhouetted against the pulsing, crimson heat.

And the screams coming from that blaze are human; there can be no doubt about that. I start to cry, in fear and horror; and my hands are shaking as I try to pull on my jeans. I run down the stairs, stagger as I haul on my Wellingtons, and I run. I run to where I can hear the voices calling, by the well.

Mammy is there, heaving up a brimming bucket. Her face is pulled tight with exhaustion, and she says automatically, "What are you doing out of bed?" I say, "What shall I do to help?" Her face quivers as she says, "Join the line, over yonder." I run up the farmyard and I see that everyone is lined up between the well and the sow house, passing buckets along, back and forth. I run and stand next to Nuala. "Nuala, what's happened?" She wipes her hair from her forehead and replies briefly. "The sow house is on fire, and the poor sow is in there, God help her, with her bonhams." The sound of the screams is writhing and curdling in spine-chilling waves. It sounds exactly like a human being under torture, unspeakable torture.

We work there for hours. Long after the sow's screaming abruptly stops, we work. I am shaking with cold and fright. We have to work to save the whole yard from going up, to stop the fire from chasing along the roof beams and to keep it from the hay barn too.

My uncles are at the rain barrels by the chicken house, pumping water up from them. The hoses are too short to reach the well from there, so the whole night is a daze of aching backs and screaming shoulders as we swing in the rhythm of passing full pails one way, empty ones the other. Granny stands by the well, her long silver plait hanging down to her waist, passing the empty buckets to Mammy all through the night. Nuala and Mammy sometimes urge her to go back into the house, but she will not leave. Are her eyes full of another fire, half a century before?

And long after the sow has stopped her screaming, we can hear her still. The sound is blazing in our ears, above the crackling of the flames as they snatch at the burning timbers. We are all white with the horror of knowing that she was burned alive, she and all her babies. We saved everything else, the hay barn included, but we are heavy with the knowledge that we have failed the sow. I don't think any of us will ever forget that.

They told us so much about hell at school and at church. Burning, burning flames eating your flesh forever. The evil stench, forever. Infinity, spent screaming in agony. And when you die, it is forever. I cannot think straight, with these thoughts of forever and forever.

The chickens didn't bother me so much, but the poor sow and her babies . . . I can't get them out of my head. The poor sow screaming, watching her babies burn around her, feeling the searing heat turn her body into one loud howl of agony. They were born so recently, and now they are dead. I saw them being born, and then I was there when they died. The sow was Granny's friend. The safety lamp that kept the babies warm at night tipped over. And the straw caught fire. The smell of her flesh . . . my stomach heaves at the thought of roast pork or frying bacon.

Mammy is furious. John cries over his roast chicken, the brown skin crisply gleaming on the white flesh. "You ungrateful little brat!" she shouts, and slaps him round the head. "When we were your age, sure we doted on a bit of meat, any chance we got!"

I won't eat the meat either. All I can see is her poor charred carcass. Mammy shouts at me, "I might have known! It was you put him up to it!" But it wasn't. Anne slurps on her chicken bones, glancing at me smugly. She is sucking the greasy black marrow from them as she crunches, dangling bits of skin from her fork.

I eat potatoes. Clean food, mashed creamy with butter. But I can hardly swallow. When we die, it is forever. So why waste time? Why not get it over with soon?

❧ Thirty

Lying in the big bed, gone to bed early. I cannot bear it with my eyes closed, and yet it's worse when I open them. The curtain opposite is swelling inward, oozing on and on toward me. I close my eyes and try not to scream.

Below me, in the kitchen, I can hear all the usual comforting sounds of evening, to-ing and fro-ing, slamming doors and clattering pans. Men's voices rumble, and chair legs scrape as someone moves nearer the fire. There is only the thickness of the floorboards between them and me. One heavy boot is tapping out a reel. Mammy and Nuala raise their voices in a wave of laughter. They'll be drinking stout and smoking cigarettes around the fire. I bid my lurching head be quiet as I try to draw comfort from these little sounds.

But it's no use. It's futile to carry on regardless. We all go in the end. Dadda is dead and his ceiling mocks me with its sneaky angles. He knows. Why eat? Why wash? All that stupid talk downstairs, all that laughter. Why bother even getting up?

• • •

But in the morning, they all get up and so do I. Have I got any choice, after all? I walk into the kitchen and pick up a chair. The back falls off in my hand. When I lift the egg saucepan from the fire, it jumps and springs from its handle. Boiling water leaps at me; I tread on crushed eggshells; egg yolk trickles down the walls. When the doorknob comes off in my hand, I go back to bed. Enough is enough. I go to bed in broad daylight. And I shan't ever get up again.

I shall stay in bed. I shall not waste time. I shall live inside my head until the time comes for my body to die. The statue is pure white in the daylight. Clear and cool. My head is thumping, hot and swollen. My spirit is invisible inside my skull. It stares out through my eyes, as still and clear as water. And when I close them, it travels on horseback, weightless over the ground, to a place where magic rules. Sweet, fresh, swooping magic is what I choose. Away from all this chaos and confusion, forever.

I don't need food. My jug of water lasts me the whole day through.

When Mammy stands at the foot of the bed in the mornings and shouts at me, I turn my face to the wall. She tries to drag me from the bed, but I go limp and don't struggle. I am transparent and nothing can hold me.

🐚 Thirty-one

How many days have I spent like this? One, or two or three?

In the mornings I am determined. I am opposing Mammy's rigid mouth and Anne's darting eyes, and sooner or later I win and am left alone. But the afternoons are beginning to get longer, it seems. My body is restless, and the clear light escapes me. But I will not get up. I am determined.

And now Nuala has come in. She does not try to find my eyes, and I am glad. I am still ashamed before her. She puts a book on the chest of drawers beside me. "When I was lonely in New York, this book was my friend," she murmurs, and goes out before I have a chance to reject it.

And so the afternoons begin to fill up again. Where does her friend take me? Between its covers, I take sips from Tir na N'Og. The land of eternal youth, hidden inside the mountains.

I lie back against the pillows, and I climb onto the back of my horse, with no saddle or bridle, just a silken halter. I ride across the fields to the cave at the base of Mount Leinster. I bend my head as bats fly in fluttering swoops from the low roof, and I stop by the blank wall at the end, deep inside the mountain. Water is trickling like crystal over the mossy stone. I close my eyes and bow my head, and water splashes over my hair.

When I open my eyes again, we are there, the horse and I. We are in the land where blossoms tumble and drift in the air, and where the sky is blue and clear. The flowers swoop from the hedgerows like birds, and the birds perched on the branches of the trees are as bright as flowers. We are weightless, the horse and I, and we leave no footprints. I reach up my hand and food drops into it from the trees. Peaches, cherries, berries: they grow the whole year through. If it rains here, it is only when the people want the colors to grow brighter, and if the wind blows, it is only when everyone is inside, warm in bed, enjoying the sound of it rattling the windowpanes.

It is Niamh who is the ruler of this land, Niamh of the golden hair, with her slow and gentle smile. She untangles problems like the thread she spins from the snaggled yarns on her distaff. She rules this land inside the mountains, the land of Tir na N'Og.

Inside the covers of Nuala's book I find a very ancient Ireland of long ago. It was a land of heroes and giants who carved the landscape with their footsteps, so huge were they. And with pebbles dropped from their pockets they made the mountains grow. Oisin was the fine young son of a giant chieftain, but he left the land of the mortals and went to join Niamh, for a spell, in her magic kingdom.

How he must have loved it there, in the freshness and peace! But even so, after a time, he grew homesick for the land of his father, and so he asked Niamh's permission to leave her for a visit home. "I give you my permission," she said, "and you may take my white horse to carry you. But beware, for if once your feet touch the earth, you will never be able to come back to me here."

So Oisin took heed of her words and rode out on her horse to the land of Ireland. But to his surprise, the land seemed to have become strangely shrunken, and all the people in it seemed to have shrunk too, so that they were giants no longer but quiet and docile little folk. He realized how weak they had become when he came upon a group of twenty of them who were trying to move a rock from the middle of a field so that they could plow it. His heart was moved by compassion as he watched them heaving and sweating from their labors. Twenty men struggling to do what one could have done with one finger, the last time he was here!

So he rode up to them and said, "Let me help you." They stood back in amazement at the radiance of his face, at the beauty of Niamh's horse. And he bent down from the saddle to scoop up the rock in one of his hands. But oh, though he was weightless and so was the horse, the rock was only too solid, and its heavy bulk was too much for the girth of his saddle, which snapped and dropped him to the ground.

And then there was cause for the people to wonder even more, for no sooner had Oisin's feet touched the earth than he shrank before their very eyes. From being an upright young giant, as supple as a beech tree, he shrank and shrank until he was a shriveled, bent old man.

And so he never more returned to Tir na N'Og. Instead, he was taken to Saint Patrick by the people, and he told the saint his story, and the tales of his father's court of heroes, and the tale of Niamh and the land of Tir na N'Og. Which is how come I am able to read it now.

It was not safe from that moment on for Niamh to visit Ireland again, for those first Irish people had lost their land, and their past had shrunk behind them. A foreign power stalked the hills and crushed the light and subtle magic underfoot. This magic lingered on in secret, written in messages on the stones, in the bubbling water, and in the whispering trees. But even so, many of the people became small and lost, and hungry and afraid.

So Niamh and her people stayed underground, except for one night of the year, when they came out and danced in the moonlight. And as their light footsteps skimmed the earth of Ireland, they danced for the day when the land would be free again. For the day when the foreign power would be washed away, so that the people could be as free as the stones, the rivers, and the trees once more. For the day when the people would have their past restored to them, and when no one but they would have the right to write their future.

✒ Thirty-two

When Mammy comes into the bedroom, I feel myself become tight all over. She fires desperate questions at me, so that my magic land recedes and her anxiety replaces it, clawing at me. When she pulls back the curtains and says, "It's a grand day!" I know that it's an accusation, and what she really means is, "Why aren't you out in the sunshine?"

She confuses me so much, with her code of words that mean different things from what they actually say. My head loses its lightness and clarity when I'm with her, so that I find myself hurling words at her like cannonballs. And before I know where I am, I am struggling in tangled threads and I don't even known myself any longer what it is I'm trying to say.

But when Nuala comes in, she just slips in quietly and tidies things away. She says very little, but what she says is very clear and simple. Today she brings me some flowers in a little jug. The jug is white with tiny multi-colored birds on it, their wings outstretched. The flowers are wildflowers, from the hedgerows. Sitting on the chest of drawers beside my bed, they look so beautiful.

Nuala is taking down the curtains at the windows. They need a wash, she says. I'm amazed at how she accepts the daily chores of housekeeping and never seems to resent them. She has brought some clean curtains with her to replace the old ones with.

She smiles at me as she says, "Mary, would you mind if I sat on your bed to thread these onto the wire?" She's holding out the new curtains and the springy brass wires which she's unthreaded from the old ones. I pull my legs up under me to make room for her and say, "No, of course I don't. Feel free."

She settles down and I watch her as she patiently eases the wire along inside the hem at the top of a curtain. "What's the point in doing that?" I say, annoyed at her quiet involvement in her task. She looks up at me, her eyebrows arching in surprise, and her mouth ripples in a smile.

"Sure, Mary, even I can't get curtains to hang at a window of their own accord! They need a bit of mechanical assistance, you know." She's waving the wire at me, teasing me. Despite myself, I smile. "I know *that*," I say. "But what's the point of changing the curtains at all?"

"Sure, them others is dirty," she answers. "Why wouldn't I change them?" "But why bother?" I insist. "Why bother with all these jobs day after day, over and over again?"

She doesn't dismiss me. She's looking at me seriously. "Well sure, Mary, even the birds of the air build their nests, and even the badgers of the fields change their bedding every day."

I lean over to her, my voice urgent. "Yes, Nuala, but why? Why does everyone bother, since they're all going to die one day?" My voice is harsh. I'm almost scared of what I'm saying.

Nuala swallows and lowers her eyes. Time stands still as I dare her to fob me off. She raises her head and leans it back, so that her throat is a lovely, pure white arc. Then she sighs and turns her head to me.

"So you've realized you're going to die one day, have you, allanah?" she murmurs to me gently. The air is very still around us as I feel the yawning pit of death clawing at my heart, turning my stomach inside out. Forever and forever! The thought of my own death is thudding in my belly, as dark and heavy as lead, as dull and imponderable as the thick shadows under the bed. And I'm so scared.

My tears start to fall in splashes and I am heaving with sobs. I am so relieved that I can cry, so frightened of crying in front of her, so terrified of death, so certain that no one will ever be able to comfort me again. I am crying for the lost days of childhood, when Mammy used to kiss my tears away and say, "It's all right, Mary. Everything will be all right in the end." I used to believe her then, but now I know that she was lying; nothing is turning out all right, and in the end there is only death.

The mattress is swaying beneath me and Nuala is next to me. Her arms are round me, holding me so tightly. My tears are falling down onto my hands, which lie helplessly, palms upward, on my knees. "I just don't understand it, Nuala." My voice is shaking through my tears. "Dadda is dead, and it's as though he never lived at all, and the sow died so horribly and her babies had only just been born, and I don't know why; it's all so cruel, so cruel. What is the point in me doing *anything* if it's all going to end one day? And every single thing I do is wrong anyway. Oh, I can't bear it."

Nuala is holding my head, stroking my tangled hair, rocking me slowly back and forth. She's leaning her cool forehead against my neck, she's pressing her cheek against my face, she's kissing me softly where the tears have streaked my skin. And I am sobbing as though a dam has burst inside me, so that all my grief is rushing out. Water is streaming from my eyes and snot is pouring from my nose. I feel as though my whole body has been loosened from its tight moorings, to be washed in huge waves of relief.

Nuala moves away slightly, still holding me, and twisting a little she pulls her hanky from her pocket. She passes it to me so simply. There is no shame between us, and I feel no embarrassment at my snotty nose, at my swollen face, at the ugly yellow heads of my spots. She's kissed me, spots and all; there are no secrets between us.

"You're going to die, and you do nothing right, so why not get it all over with? Oh yes, I know, I know, whisht now, allanah, I know." Nuala's voice is a long, low keening at my sorrow. "I feel it too, and the first time was the worst. We are born, and we will die, and we're alone both times, and so what is the point of doing anything in the middle? Anything at all, when it's all so hard." Rocking me, she is giving voice to my thoughts so exactly that I know she really has felt them too.

"I ask myself, Mary, does the sun think that when the storms are raging? Do the trees think that when the leaves are stripped from their branches in the winter? Can one cloud obliterate the whole sky? Or is there someplace somewhere that the sun is shining? If you look out from the shadows, everything is dark. Move into the sun, and all the colors of creation lighten."

Cradled in her arms, I think of the buds on the trees in spring. They seem so frail, so tremulous and tender, but they are charged with a mighty force. I think of the clouds passing over the fields, while her voice soothes me like a chant.

"Like a horse with blinkers on, standing in the shadows, you can see nothing else. But it's there, allanah, all around you. No need to run and hide from the darkness, for it will pass, like night into day. And your eyes have seen it all now, the darkness as well as the light. There's nothing more to fear."

We are sitting side by side, in silence. The things we are talking of are the things that cannot be denied. Just to talk about them with someone else has wiped away the darkness, the prison of secret dread. I am not alone, cradled in her warmth. My eyes are on the flowers that she brought me. Little flowers, delicate and lovely, that grow each year in the hedgerows, whether anyone notices them or not. Their petals curve and touch, like Nuala's head and mine. I could spend my life trying to draw anything as beautiful as that and get nowhere. And in a few days they will wither and die ... but they'll come up each year anyway, I know.

☙ Thirty-three

I'm still staying in bed up here, but the terror is leaving. I want to stay in this peace a while longer, with the clean sheets and the flowers and Nuala's book. And my thoughts, too. I am so grateful to Nuala, though she waved her hand at me when I tried to thank her. "Thank me?" she said. "We're all in it together." But I'm not sure what she meant by that.

And I realize that I have done nothing to help her; I haven't even given a thought to her request for help, ages ago it seems, before this nightmare began. What would I say to her American children if she had them? I can't think of anything, and I'm so scared that I will fail her. But when I look at the flowers, they settle me. They remind me to let things pass and take their course.

I'm reading Nuala's book, going back into the world of ancient Ireland's history, and I'm delighted to have found the story of Maeve, or Mebh as it is written in the Irish way. Mary is my first name, but Maeve is my second, and though I know a lot about Mary, the Mother of God, I know nothing about Maeve. So I'm excited as I read this story, the story of the first Maeve.

Maeve was a queen, the only one in Ireland. She ruled over the province of Connaught, when all the others were ruled over by kings. She had everything that she needed; fine lands and cattle, a palace rich with gold and silver, loyal women to help her, and strong soldiers of both sexes to fight with her, should she ever be threatened by attack. But no one ever did attack her, for they all knew that she was mighty and warlike in battle, driving her own chariot and wielding her own battle-ax. She was also more graceful and more generous hearted than any other woman in Ireland at that time.

The one thing she didn't have was a husband, although all the kings of Ireland came to her, or sent their sons, to ask for her hand in marriage. But Maeve said, "Why should I have a husband? I can have any man I fancy, without the bother of marrying him."

She saw that a strong woman like herself would need a strong man to be her husband. She saw that a husband could give her nothing that she didn't have already in the way of wealth or power. So she asked all the men who came to woo her one question: "Are you strong enough for me to take as a husband?" And she was not talking of strength of body, or of riches or of power, but of spirit.

She looked at these men as they came, and she asked of them nothing but the absence of meanness, of jealousy, and of cowardice. She wanted a man who was her equal in bravery, in grace, and in generosity—so that he would not be forever resenting these qualities in her.

She did not want to be greater than her husband: what she did want was that he should acknowledge *her* as *his* equal, with love and with respect.

Eventually, she found a man whom she believed had all these qualities, and she married him, in a free and equal spirit. His name was Ailil, and she truly believed he was free of envy or meanness. But oh, it was a sad thing, for no sooner had she married him than he started in on his boasting, saying to her, "You're much better off since you married the likes of me. The woman who marries me has the benefit of my wealth and position. You should be grateful for this."

He wouldn't shut up, and Maeve was appalled at his meanness of spirit. So she challenged him to a contest, because in the end this was the only argument he seemed to understand, to prove that she was equal to him and he to her. And this is how one of the longest and bloodiest wars in ancient Ireland began, lasting years and dragging whole clans into it, because Maeve refused to give in.

The story of the war is long and confused and messy, and I can't even find out whom seems to have won in the end. But the thing that interests me is this. Mammy named me after Maeve, but did she know this story at the time? The story of Maeve who was so brave and fearless and wouldn't back down for the sake of peace, but stuck to her true beliefs through thick and thin? If this is what Mammy wanted for me, she has a dead funny way of showing it, is all I can say.

Mary, now. Mary the Blessed Virgin, pure and mild: *she's* more like my mother's hopes for me. Cross-legged on the bed, I gaze at her outstretched hands on the mantelpiece. They are like the hands of the woman printed on the sheets. The way they stand is the same, Mary and the woman from the flour sacks. Except that Mary is pale and luminous, and this woman is blazing in the radiant light of the sun.

I don't avoid her eyes anymore, this statue. Her pale light has helped me these past hot and anguished days, like moonlight on the water. And Nuala's cool hand has helped me too, soothing the black claws from my heart. But I'm thinking of Mammy now, and of the life we lead in England, and the loneliness to come when we return. If I had the sunlight flaming in my heart, and if I was as strong as Maeve, whose name I carry, life would really be worth living.

✒ Thirty-four

Nuala has brought me up a new pair of stockings as a present! They're called Midnight Haze. They'd look lovely with my black miniskirt.

I get out of bed and try them on with it to show Nuala, and she says, "They look grand, Mary! Tell you what, why don't we go into Kilkenny this morning, just you and me? We'll have great gas, so we will!"

My heart leaps at the thought, but then it sinks again. Mammy'd never let me out of the house dressed like this. "It's all right, Nuala," I say, and quickly get undressed again and back into bed.

"What's the matter?" she's asking, all concerned. I fiddle with the stockings as I fold them up, and then throw myself back against the pillows. "Oh God, I don't know," I say. "It's just that, well, Mammy would never dream of buying me a pair of stockings, just like that, for a present. And I doubt if she'll even let me wear these while I'm here! I think she'd be happiest if I was dressed like a nun or something."

Nuala's face is looking very stern suddenly, it seems to me. "Mary," she says after a while, "you mustn't be so hard on your mother." I can't believe what I'm hearing! *Me*, hard on *her*? I feel like opening my mouth and screaming. "Nuala," I'm shouting, "I try and try and *try* to get through to Mammy. And all she ever does is avoid me, or hit me, or tell me to pray! How am I supposed to get through to someone like that?"

Nuala takes my hand. "I've been talking to your mammy, my sister Bridie," she says quietly. "Oh yes, I have. I didn't forget my promise to you. And Mary, she's been talking to me. And I'd like to tell you a little story she told me. Will you listen, if I tell it to you now?"

I suppose I have no choice, really, so I agree. But I'm full of resentment at first, until Nuala gets well into this story.

"Your mammy is a fair bit older than me, as you know, and when I was two years old, she must have been about fifteen. Our sister Shelagh, whom you've never met, the one that's in Australia now, she's only a couple of years older than me. And then there were all our brothers, of a variety of ages. But Bridie was the eldest girl, and so she was supposed to be in charge of all us younger ones.

"All through the summer months, she used to do a full day's work from dawn till dusk. The schools were all closed, because it's the busiest time of year for the farmers, the summertime, and all the children are needed at home to help. But Bridie had all the work of looking after us to do, as well as the work around the yard and in the fields.

"So anyway, one morning she was walking past the open stable door at milking time, when what do you think she saw? The bright colors of my little frock, down there where they should not have been. On the stable floor, among the horses' hooves! Sure God, Bridie was near killed with the shock! She stopped in her tracks so suddenly that the two full pails of milk she was carrying slopped milk all down her sides. Sweat was plastering her hair to her forehead, but what she saw on that stable floor made her body tremble with cold.

"My sister Bridie was always terrible scared of horses, do you see. She'd seen the big bay stallion go wild one day, out in the yard while Dadda was leading him on a long rein, and she'd heard the dreadful crunch as his hoof broke Dadda's thigh. She's never trusted a horse since that time.

"But she was also supposed to be keeping an eye on her little sisters—that's to say, myself and Shelagh—and so she had another fear to contend with that morning as well. She knew that if I was on the floor of the stable, and something awful happened to me, then it would be she herself, and no one else, who'd get the blame for it.

"And so it was that she shivered in the warm sunlight that morning. She dumped the two buckets onto the ground, never minding the big slops that whooshed out of them as she did so, nor the fact that the cats would surely come slinking toward them from their lookouts on the wall as soon as her back was turned.

"As she ran quietly into the shadows of the stable, she

could feel Dadda's anger stinging her ears and the backs of her legs. And the heart in her thumped in her ears as she tried to make out a sense of what was going on in that dim, dark place. Four mares were in there, all huge, all of them in foal. The heat had made them irritable. They were stirring and stamping their feet and horse-flies were making them shudder.

"At first, all that Bridie could see was a shifting, dark mass of bodies and a kind of mist of buzzing horseflies. But the sound of the metal shoes grating on the con-crete floor made her look down through the mass of legs to find where I was lying. There was a beam of light slanting across the floor. It was skimming the straw and a corner of it was touching the bright flowers of my frock. Bridie crouched down, trying to see exactly what I was up to, and where exactly I was.

"And sure Jaysus, she was almost killed with panic when she finally saw me! Wasn't I lying with my two fat arms wrapped around one of the hooves! And hadn't I placed my head right on the long white hairs of the mare's fetlock! And wasn't I sleeping, cozy as a baby chick, with my cheek nuzzling the hoof itself!

"Poor Bridie! She did her level best to attract my at-tention, without startling the mare. She was so scared that the horse would shift and crush my head, like an egg, beneath her hoof. So, even though she was terrified of horses, what did she do but start to crawl along that floor on her belly!

"It must have cost her a lot, that long, slow crawl.

The mares were blowing loudly and shaking their huge heads or rubbing them low against their knees to fend off the flies. The noise and all the agitated movements must have terrified her, sure. But she managed to keep going, to get to the legs of the farthest mare, and then edge her way forward to the front hoof, where I lay sleeping all oblivious. Bridie stopped then and waited, trying to work out what to do. Sweat and gritty hay-seeds and bits of straw were pasting her arms and her legs and she rubbed her head up and down her arm to wipe her forehead. 'Sure, what in the name of God will I do?' she whispered into her arm.

"There was nothing for it but to go straight ahead and disentangle me from the mare. So, summoning all her courage, Bridie stretched forward and gently un-wound my arms from around the hoof. Then she grabbed me firmly round the waist, pulled me with all her strength, and rolled sideways away from the mare toward the feeding manager. The two of us tumbled into the straw in the nick of time, and the mare jerked back with a start, out of her drowsy trance.

"I was grizzling and wriggling, squirming and pro-testing in Bridie's arms, and the mare was whickering with her ears back. Bridie squeezed me tighter and gave me a shake, hissing, 'Whisht now, Nuala, and be glad you're saved! Look at the state of your good dress, all covered in muck! Come along out of here now or I'll tell Dadda, and he'll get the strap to you, so he will!'

"Myself, I don't remember this, Mary. Wasn't I only

a little scrap of a thing at the time. I'm just telling it as Bridie told me, mind. Well, next thing was, she pushed me along the back wall, scrabbling along behind me, and then across to the door on all fours. And then she scooped me up and stumbled out with me into the dazzling sunshine. She was stunned by the sudden glare of the sun, and screwed up her eyes to get her bearings. And it was only then that she remembered the two full pails of milk going to waste where she'd left them earlier!

"She dumped me down onto the ground and ran to fetch the buckets. But before she reached them, she was stunned by a blow from Dadda's hand. She couldn't work out what was happening for a minute, and it was only slowly that she could make out the sense of Dadda's voice: '. . . spilled by the frigging cats! Lookit! Two pailfuls gone to waste! And you idling your time away, off in there! You're a waster, so y'are! Come here with me till I get the strap to you!'

"As he undid his belt, she did try to explain, but Dadda only hit her harder for telling lies. His temper was up. She was to blame, and that was that. Sure I was mortified when your mammy told me this tale that I wasn't old enough to stick up for her! I must have just toddled off to play somewhere else, I suppose, leaving her to face the music on her own. Anyway, when the belting was over, your mammy said, she just went back to the cow house and carried on with her work. But I expect she must have sat there for a while, crying quietly into the warm flank of the cow she should have been milking."

And when later Nuala leaves me I bury my head in the pillows and cry too. I keep thinking of how Mammy was really a young girl once, like me, and of how lonely she must have been.

✎ Thirty-five

When I wake up this morning, I feel hot and clammy with sweat. I can tell that it is early because there are no sounds in the house, and I wonder what it is that has woken me up. Then I feel the familiar pains in my belly and thighs, and the wetness between my legs. My period again! I sit up and decide there and then to have a bath, before anyone else is awake.

I take my dressing gown and slip out of the room. The kitchen is full of its early morning secrets and of all the unknown things that have been happening in it while I've been upstairs. The kettles are whispering softly over the fire. I lift one and carry it into the back kitchen carefully, feeling the blood trickling down my leg.

I mix some water in the little tin bath; not too much of the hot morning water from the kettle, plenty of cold from the bucket. But it's just right, not too hot and not too cold. I wash carefully and thoroughly. It is so lovely to wash the sweat from my skin and from my itchy matted hair.

When I am dry and clean and wrapped in my dressing

gown, I stand outside in the sunshine drying my hair. I feel so happy, clean and fresh and new, in the light of the sun. When Granny comes down, I am so pleased to see her that I run to her and give her a hug. She's pleased to see me too; she laughs and calls me a good girl. I shove some Wellingtons on and run to the well to refill the bucket I've almost used up. And Granny doesn't stop me, but thanks me with a smile, and we carry the bath outside and pour the water away.

As I watch it soak into the warm concrete of the yard, people seem to arrive from all directions. Billy ambles out, rubbing his face with a towel, and Pat-Joe and my cousins are coming up the lane toward the gate. The haymaking must be beginning today, then! But I don't feel quite ready to face anyone, not yet. So I slip back into the house and run up the stairs.

From the window, I can see Orla and Carmel and Siobhan down below, throwing their arms around Mammy, eyeing up Anne and John. They're chattering like birds, pestering Mammy. "Where's Mary? Ah go on, Bridie, tell us. Where's Mary got to?" I see Mammy's face lose its brightness as she steps back from them, her eyes glancing up to this window. She murmurs something to them, and they all follow her out of the yard.

My heart is tugging me as I blink my eyes to shut away that glimpse of Mammy's face. And my cousins too; I've been wanting to see them for so long. But I know I'm not quite ready yet to go down and join the farm. They'll be here now for a while, until the hay is all in. And for the moment I know I still need to be on my own.

I think to myself, they call her Bridie. And they throw their arms around her. And she told her story to Nuala, not to me. And the sun is climbing higher up the sky.

Now Granny and Billy are below in the yard. Granny is tethering the gray mare to the trap to take the dinners to everyone in the fields. I could be helping her. Billy is leading the young unbroken colt into the yard from the near meadow. They are talking quietly to each other.

"It's shocking warm, thanks be to God," says Granny.

"Sure, I'm murthered in the heat," replies Billy.

"Will you put that lad in the shade; the way he won't be roasted," says Granny. "Pat-Joe won't be along till a good while later, the work he has to do. So make sure you leave a drop of water for that fine lad; the way he won't be parched dry standing there."

The air is drifting in the window, heavy with the scents of all the tumbled hedgerows. It is so sweet and fresh. I am almost tingling with life. So, Pat-Joe has bought the colt from Billy! I'd love to draw him, before he goes, standing quietly tethered to the stable wall. Soon Granny and Billy are gone; there is no one about. I get dressed in a loose cotton frock and get my pencils and sketchbook. I'm excited at the thought of drawing that colt.

And when I get out into the yard, the sun beats me across the head and eyes and I am completely dazzled.

It's been so long since I was outdoors in the full heat of day! The sun shocks me, like an electric current. I stand back against the house wall, feeling the warmth soak into me, and I am dizzy with sunshine. I have to screw up my eyes to make out the shapes and colors of the world. I feel my heart singing with the simple joy of being alive. I've been upstairs in the shadows for so long.

I turn my head to the colt. He is standing against the wall under a cloud of flies. His head is hanging, his ears are back, and one of his hooves is resting on its toe. He looks so bored, so drained of freedom as he stands there, in the age-old stance of horses waiting. He reminds me of myself, when I was waiting for the end upstairs. He shakes his head to beat back the flies and flings his tail up and down, in the manner of a foal, to stop them biting the soft skin under his belly. But the flies scatter only to return immediately. Poor colt! Trapped like I was, tethered to the walls of this house.

And suddenly, all in a rush, I know that I am going to take him and ride him, off over the fields, to where the horizons shift and where other worlds begin. I run and hide my sketchbook in the stable, take a handful of oats and a supple leather halter, and then walk toward him, with my palm full of my offering of oats.

I am taking deep breaths to ease away the jagged feelings of anxiety from the air between us. He lifts his head, and it's all right. A look of kindly interest is replacing the one of boredom, and he is whiffling over my hand to pick up the oats. "There's a good boy," I mur-

mur to him, and I draw my free hand over the lovely arch of his neck, sweeping his mane from between his eyes. I press my face into the warmth of his coat and feel my excitement rise as I breathe in his smell. I whisper, "Will you let me ride you now, my darling?"

He is tall, so tall that I have to climb on top of the wall by the gate and edge him round to slip off the tatty rope halter and replace it with mine. Then, from the top of the wall, I stretch my leg across and mount him, as easily and simply as that!

🖎 Thirty-six

I can hardly believe it! On horseback at last! I feel my body settle on his back, and my legs and hands send him messages that he understands. I haven't felt so comfortable for ages. And I refuse to think things like, He's never been ridden like this before, and he's only half-broken. Broken! What a word! I won't break you, little colt. We'll go off together here, like equals, and your feet aren't heavy with shoes, and you've no cold, hard bit between your teeth.

We set off down the lane in the opposite direction from the haymaking. I know I'd be in trouble if anyone saw me. So we walk away from everyone else, between the hedgerows tumbling with the flowers of the wild rose and the bramble, and heavy with the dark, glossy clusters of sweet elderberries.

When we get to the first corner in the lane, we pause, and I look to the left. There is a gap in the ditch, with the remains of an old wall and wooden posts where a gate had once been. It is the entrance to what was once a little farm, still called "Corcorans' " after the family who used to live here. But no one lives here now. The father had sickened at the same time that England placed one of its embargoes on Irish cattle. So the family fell low, and when his daughter Anne had buried her family one by one, and slaughtered all the cattle that no one would buy, she could think of nothing but selling the land and taking a passage to join her sister in New York.

Dadda had tried to help the family; he'd sent them over sacks of flour, and he tilled and planted a field of vegetables for them. But the sickness had taken hold. And in the end it was Dadda who bought the land, giving Anne a fair price for it, at a time when it was worth nothing. His cattle are on the land now, but the dwelling house has fallen down, and tangled wild things have reclaimed the tracks of the Corcorans' carts. And the gate has rotted from its posts, to be buried by the brambles.

As I look along the track toward the house, I can see Mount Leinster in the distance. The land between me and the mountain is spread out as clearly as a painting. Hedgerows, little fields, and small pieces of woodland roll back into the foothills like a counterpane. I'll cross this landscape and make for the mountain, I decide. It doesn't seem too far away.

This track is grassy, like a roadway in Tir na N'Og, trod only by wild things and the unshod feet of ponies. The violet light, the gleam of water, the splashing water hens all have me imagining that I am Maeve herself, riding home to her rath. I can't decide whether my shelter should be a cave of stone or a house built inside a tree. Should I have leaves for my ceiling and branches for my bed, or should I have a warm cave fire with leaping shadows and fur to sleep upon? I can't quite decide. The colt veers to the left, and suddenly we are in the clearing in front of the Corcorans' dwelling house.

It is a house of stone and timber and thatch, which seems to have burrowed itself into the ground. The squat stones of its walls are patterned with moss, and the paint on the door has dried and cracked, so that it looks like ancient lichen, encrusted on the wood. The thatch has become matted and weighty and has slipped down over one corner, where the ivy is scrambling up it in a glossy, dark, berry-hung curtain. It seems as though the growing things have roofed this house from the start. The window holes are small, like two dark, unseeing eyes.

It seems strange to be walking past it, the colt and I, with no dogs giving warning of our presence and no hand slipping open the half-door to greet us. A young beech has pushed its way through the roof at the back. A tree growing inside the kitchen! The house seems to have lost all connection with people and to have allowed nature to take over completely.

And yet as we walk past it into the shadows behind it, I feel a ripple of fear. There are ghosts here, the haunting wraiths of Ireland's sorrowful past. They are whispering among the upended cooking pots rusting in the nettles. People have died here, here in this very spot.

And the rustling trees seem to be sighing with their voices.

Shivering, I turn the colt back onto the track and continue toward the mountain. I am glad of the sun upon my back. I am glad of the warm moving body of the horse against my legs. What a shame it is that Mammy is afraid of horses. I wonder if she has ever walked this way? We are descending into a wide valley, which opens out into a broad plain at the foothills of the mountain. It rolls in beauty of field and woodland, of wildness and gentleness, the forty shades of green dotted with cattle and the soft gold of ripe hay. And as we trot down the emerald green track, the face of the mountain is changing all the time. It is growing much clearer too, and I can see the folds of its crevices, and the rich mantle of green that is climbing in forests up its sides.

Tall trees touch the sky on either side of us, like vast explosions of life. When people built cathedrals, they must have imitated trees, the way they grow with huge vertical pillars and spreading tracery. But when Maeve lived in this land, her people worshiped in the canopies of the forests and gave each letter in their alphabet the name of a tree. And when they lost their land, they wrote their spells and songs of sadness and hope in the leaves and branches. And at this moment the air is alive with their voices.

A language of air in the leaves, of water on stones, of wood tap-tapping on wood in the living branches is in my ears. And the warmth of the sun is bathing us all. How long have I ridden in this soft land of beckoning trees? It feels like forever, but the mountain is no nearer. I stop to let the colt drink from the small runnel beside the track. The whole landscape is shifting and changing all the time, and yet the mountain is no nearer. Perspectives are shifting and the perfumed breezes are filling my head. The colt blows a spray of droplets from his nose, edging back from the water. In the racing beck among the stones, water turns white where it leaps into the air.

I am dreamy and spellbound. The elusive magic of Tir na N'Og is all around me, and inside me too. The whole land is alive with it. The cattle in the field beyond, lifting their heads as we pass, are like fairy cattle, belly-high in wild flowers and grasses. The mountain is changing color again. Two small wispy clouds are hanging gaily over its summit.

My belly is heavy and warm with my period. I clench and unclench my legs against the muscles of the colt. I am making my body work after so long. And it is working in rhythm with the colt. I have trusted him, and he has been so willing on this warm ride. So he must trust me, too. He must sense no fear in me, because I have trusted myself to ride him.

I am strong and calm. There is no distance between me and everything surrounding me. I can almost feel Dadda, out there in the fields he rode through nearly every day. He is dead, and one day I too will die, but we are part of something out there, something that has given the miracle of life to these trees, this land, these flowers, and the warm pulse inside our skin. There is no ending; everything is continuing. The whole land is alive, and the air above it.

A flight of geese—or are they swans, with their long necks questing like pennants?—is parting the sky and veering across our path. They land in a field ahead of us, with much uproar. The ducks by the beck are answering them and clattering up into the air. The colt snorts. Two tiny wrens flitter across the lane ahead of us. This real world that we are passing through is the same as the one of my dreams. And the geese, the ducks, the wrens—they are all telling us to turn back.

I have seen enough. I know now that it takes longer than an afternoon to reach a mountain. And that the land of your dreams might be the very one you're walking through. Curling my fingers in the tangle of his mane, I turn the colt back on himself and head for home.

❧ Thirty-seven

Riding back, enchanted, on his warm, rolling back, with my bare legs dangling, I feel feasted and full. I am full of the lilting songs of trees and mountain, and the trill of water flowing over stones. When we pass by Corcorans' again, I pause, and silently pay homage to the yearning ghosts. Wrenched from this magic land, they have returned to haunt it from the thickets. From the shadows they are telling me that I owe my life to them. That my strength and health are conjured from centuries of struggle in the air around me.

A spell is weaving around me, from the heat of the sun, from the stones of the walls, from the green moss, the plaited thatch and the hewn wood, from the flight of the geese on the air, and from the moorhen splashing in the water. It is a spell of completeness, of the past weaving thanks and praises into hope for the future. And I hold it in my heart as I turn and follow the track home. It tells me that I am luckier than any of the people who have gone before me. I do not have to work all my days in a numbing battle against poverty and sickness, in a struggle to bring up children in a world that denies them even food or warmth. I do not have to be a victim of circumstance. And it asks me gently, What am I going to do with this much richness, this much luck?

I feel as excited as I did the first morning here, when the whole world seemed spread out for me to run through. But that time, so long ago it seems, I lost it all. And will I lose it all again? I'm bound to get a telling-off when I get back. Will everything explode again then, like last time? Will I feel the wild waves of anger and resentment buffeting my head again?

My heart jolts for a second, but the spell bounces it back up again. It is nudging me, this spell, poking my arm like an elf. What's it saying? I strain my eyes and ears to the utmost, trying to catch it. Maeve is saying, "Let me be your equal." Yes, that's it! I have a choice. I do not have to be a victim of circumstances, of my parents' anger, or of anybody's expectations for me! I decided to take to my bed, and now I have decided to get up. I did that, and now I can decide to show them all that I am capable of making sensible decisions. The colt has come to no harm.

As we turn from the track and turn into the lane, I look back and say "Thank you." Then I see our house above the trees ahead of me. And as we start to trot down the lane, my heart is singing with its first real song of freedom.

I am laughing with the happiness of my last gay trot down the lane when I turn into the yard. My heart lurches as I see Pat-Joe come out of the stable. Uh-oh, I might be in for it now! But let's see how I can face it out. I slip off the colt's back and nuzzle his neck, thanking him for the ride and summoning up my confidence for what might lie ahead. He curves his head around me, touching my shoulder with his nose, like a good omen.

Nuala is laughing. "Sure Jaysus, did you see the setup of her, Pat? Tell me now, who does that remind you of?"

"She has Dadda's back, and the hold of his hands on the reins," says Pat-Joe. He reaches and takes the reins from me. "Grand lass yourself, Mary." He smiles. "Tell me now, did I do right to buy this lad?"

"Yes, you did," I reply. My voice is clear and strong, with no apology. "He's a fine young horse, with no malice or vices in him at all. You won't need to break him. Only show him what you want, and he'll do his best to get it right." Pat-Joe is running his hand along each of the colt's forelegs. "It's glad I am of your opinion." He twinkles. "You have Dadda's feel for a horse, right enough."

He hasn't even mentioned the fact that I've taken and ridden the colt without permission! He springs up and mounts him and looks down at us. "Well, I'll be on me way now, so. We'll say no more about this, and no one'll be any the wiser." Nuala laughs and puts her arm round me. "Good luck now, Pat," says Nuala, waving him away.

She turns me round and we walk back, through the lengthening shadows in the yard, to the house. And not a word does she say to me about the whole affair. Her eyes are warm as she teases me instead. "Well now, Mary, so you're up and about again, are you! We'd better see if we can find a few old jobs to do about the house, now hadn't we, to make up for all the work you've missed out on!"

I pull away from her and she lunges at my ribs with her tickling hands, so that we enter the house shrieking and giggling, and quite at one with the world.

❧ Thirty-eight

Feeling so full of energy now, I'm up before anyone except Granny. I sing as I help her. In my song, there is the long dark dirge of the shadows behind the Corcorans' house, and then the spirals and trills of dancing sunlight, water trickling over stones, and the wrens darting over the hedgerows. Then the long, dark dirge again, and then the tra-la trill again. And so on, as we work.

Orla and Carmel come laughing into the kitchen. I'm so glad to see them at last! Two girls to talk to. Orla goes with me into the back kitchen and whispers, "So you had great sport with the colt, I hear!" I look at her defensively, thinking of Anne and betrayal and being in trouble, but her eyes are dancing merrily with nothing more than the sharing of a scrape. I laugh and say, "Oh Orla, isn't it great to go off for a ride on your own?" "It is so," she agrees, "and will you be coming down to the fields today?" "Oh yes," I say, "will you?" "I will indeed," she says. "Do you want to come and give a look over the new tractor I'm after bringing down for Billy?" Surprised, I look at her. I'm surprised that Billy has actually bought the tractor so soon, and surprised that it is Orla who has driven it here from the merchants in Kilkenny.

I go out with her. She has a strong long stride in her walk. Her hair is thick and curly, and her face is open and fresh. I ask, "Why did *you* bring it here?" And she explains, "Well, sure Daddy can't drive it yet, and I'm after having plenty of practice over at Whelan's. I was over there a lot this past month, helping with the drainage on his five meadows. I'll have to show Billy how to use it, but there's little to it, sure."

She takes me out of the yard to the gateway of the near meadow. And there it is, a brand-new Fordson Major, high upon its massive back wheels. She springs up onto the seat and starts it up. She handles the levers and gears lightly and nimbly and turns the wheel easily in one hand as she backs it up, looking over her shoulder. Her bare legs are tanned and scratched.

I feel very proud of my cousin as she takes the big machine a short way up the lane, maneuvers it skillfully to turn it round, back and forth, back and forth, between the ditches, and then back to where I'm standing. She turns off the engine, and looking down at me she says, "This yoke and its like will make an awful big difference to the farmers, and that's the truth. Billy will till his fields in no time this year!"

I don't answer her. I'm too busy looking up at her with admiration, my cousin Orla with her small hands, able to drive a big machine like that. I say as much to her, and she shrugs her shoulders. "Ah well," she says, jumping down to join me, "is it not only an old machine! There's a lot more skill in driving a pair of horses, or in riding an unridden colt for that matter!" She winks at me, and we walk back to the house.

Orla and I are chasing each other down the lane, toward the fields where the hay has been cut. Everyone helps with the haymaking, even Anne and Daddy. And John's foot is fine, so he's out there with the lark. The meadows are full of people: our whole family, and the Kinsellas and Nolans from down the lane. Everyone helps everyone else until all the hay is in. It's like a race, while the good weather lasts.

The meadows are ringing with talk and laughter as we dash in at the gateway. Mammy is in her element, larking about and catching up on a whole year's news with the neighbors. Us kids are supposed to work together.

"Orla!" I pant, bumping into her as she slows down. "Can I work with you?" "You can, o' course," she says, handing me a pitchfork. John, Anne, Siobhan, and Carmel are raking, gathering the hay from its cut rows into piles. But Orla and I will work together, making haycocks.

Using our pitchforks, we spear into the raked piles and build them into neat, round haycocks. I have to pause often because my back, shoulders, and arms are not used to such hard work. But Orla never seems to tire. She works with a loose and easy rhythm that I much admire, her body bending and stretching with ease. It is demanding work, thrusting the sharp prongs of the forks into clumps of hay and then pitching these forkfuls ever higher to form a compact, well-constructed haycock.

"I'm surprised you didn't want to work with Anne," says Orla, wiping hayseeds from her face with the back of her hand. I don't reply. Orla leans on her fork, scanning the field and the blue sky with pleasure. "Mind you," she adds, "it does work best like this. Sure she can work with Carmel, and John can work with Siobhan, and I can work with you. That way, we're all well matched." "I don't know so much about that!" I laugh as my shoulders wrench in midtoss, and I collapse, scattering a forkful of hay around me. Orla helps me up.

"Do you not get on with Anne?" she asks. I'm startled, but I try to tell the truth. "Not really," I reply. "Oh, I don't know. I hardly know her, really, even though she is my sister." "But do you not do things together, like?" quizzes Orla curiously. "N-no, we don't," I mumble. Orla is looking at me as though I'm a very strange specimen. "It's different in England, Orla." I stick to my guns. "There's nothing like this, all out in the fields together, and we're in different classes at school. She has her own friends, and I ..." I turn my head away. "Well, anyway, we don't go out together anywhere, or anything like that. And anyway, she's younger than me." "My sisters are younger than me," muses Orla, "but we do everything together. Oh well," she sighs, "as you say, it must be different where you come from." And we carry on working together.

When we reach the top of our haycock, my arms are shrieking in protest. Orla has begun to gather hay together for the next one, but I have to rest. I see Anne over in the distance, handling her rake with a great sense of self-importance. I bet she's got her tongue out, pressed between her teeth. Periodically she pauses and seems to be giving out at John, who stumbles now and again over what he is doing. The rake is too big for him, really. Poor John! I think, but I'm not thinking of the rake.

I scan the field to find Daddy and Mammy, but I can't make either of them out. Then, to my amazement, I see Mammy running, running in my direction along the edge of the field. She is weaving and dodging among the haycocks, and then, to my astonishment, she bends down and begins to burrow herself right inside one! She doesn't stop until she's wriggled her way right inside, completely hidden in the hay. What on earth is she doing?

I look hard into the distance and see Nuala and one of the Kinsella girls, running and giggling, dodging between the rows, calling her name. "Bridie! Bridie! Sure where is she at all?" Nuala is standing in the middle of the field, looking round, and then it seems to dawn on her that Mammy must be inside one of the haycocks. She calls to Maire Kinsella, and the two of them run and grab a pitchfork each. Shrieking with delight, they are yelling, "Bridie, if you don't come out we'll spear you with a pitchfork, so we will!" And now they are beginning, with much noise, to thrust their forks into the haycocks nearest them, moving down the rows toward her.

I throw down my fork and run toward them. "Nuala! Maire! Don't!" I shout, but when I catch up with them, they are oblivious and choking with laughter. They are like two wild things. "Wait till we spear her leg!" they hoot. "Wait till we puncture her guts!" They are egging each other on, their eyes wild and blazing. "Jaysus, wait till we drag the innards out of her!"

They are bumping into each other, with tears of laughter pouring down their faces, ramming their forks into each haycock as they scream out their threats. They really do mean it! They seem to have taken leave of their senses.

I can't bear it. "Mammy! Mammy!" I cry. "Give yourself up!" I'm so scared that they'll lurch into the one she's hidden in and really hurt her. They are so tousled and disorderly, so lawless and unstoppable that I'm really frightened by them, yodeling as they lunge into the hay.

Then there is a scrambling sound and Mammy rushes out, with hay trailing from her hair and from her body. Nuala throws down her fork and belts after her, with Maire in hot pursuit, and then the three of them are rolling all together on the ground, tumbling and laughing and tickling each other Mammy's voice is hiccuping, scrambling out through her giggles. "Ah no, Nuala, will you stop, ah sure will you STOP now!"

Choking for breath, they have exhausted themselves, and they all subside and lie still. And as they lie there in a tumbled heap below me, they look like girls, all bare arms and legs and tousled hair, their dresses all pulled adrift, panting with laughter. Then they slowly clamber to their feet, brushing the hay out of each other's eyes.

Spitting on hayseeds, Mammy is turning to me. "Sure, Mary, why did you give the game away on me? Wasn't I nicely hidden where I was?" My heart lurches, but she is looking at me with her smiling eyes. And I can see that she is pleased with me, really. She turns her head back to them. "They'd never have found me, pair of eejits that they are!"

Maire and Nuala squeal at being called eejits and make a lunge at her again, but she has grabbed my hand. And she draws me with her and we scamper together over the tossed hay back toward Orla. Mammy is swinging my arm back and forth, back and forth as we run, and ahead of us Orla is swinging her loaded pitchfork into the air, singing "Hey yayy!" at the top of her lungs. And when we reach her, and tumble panting into her, a shower of gold floats softly down and glitters in the blue air around us.

❧ Thirty-nine

My heart is singing all the rest of that morning as I carry on my work with Orla. Mammy was pleased with me, and she held my hand as we ran across the fields! I'm bubbling with happiness when I see the head of the gray mare come dancing above the hedgerows. How brilliant! Granny is coming with our dinners! Everything is so perfect!

Granny turns the trap into the meadow. She's brought big crocks of steaming, flowery potatoes, their dark skins curling back to reveal the creamy white insides. And big pots of bacon and cabbage and onions, and tea in old lemonade bottles, stoppered with rags. It's all so lovely, the delicious food eaten out of doors, leaning back against the haycocks with our knives and forks and plates.

And Granny is out here too now. She sits and judges the work being done and gives her opinion, and Billy, Pat-Joe, and the Kinsella man all lean their heads respectfully toward her. Dadda's mare shakes her head inside the bridle and blinkers and eats the loose hay at her feet. It's the first haymaking since Dadda's death, and everyone is treating Granny with respect.

We all burp and relax, and listen to the talk. Anne is making posies of the little flowers dried among the hay, carefully and neatly. She is so absorbed in her delicate work, my sister. She hands the little nosegays round, and people tuck them into their buttonholes. Nuala tucks hers into the band of her ponytail. But Anne doesn't give me one. Well, I didn't expect her to, really. Then we all start back to work on Granny's say-so, first packing all the plates and pots back into their boxes and replacing them in the trap.

My shy uncle Joe has taken Anne aside. I follow them with my eyes as I slowly walk back with Orla. Is he going to show her the business of making ropes? These ropes are made of hay, and they are flung crosswise over the haycocks and then pegged into the ground all round to hold the hay in place until it's taken to the hay barn. I want to say to him, "Don't get *her* to do it! She'll only give up halfway and go running to Daddy!"

But Joe has already given her the tool, which is just a thin, hook-shaped bit of metal rammed into a short bit of broom handle. And his quiet voice is explaining to her how to use it. I stop and watch to see if she's going to show us up.

He pushes the hook into the base of the haycock and curls some hay around it. Then he tells her to hold the wooden handle, and he shows her how to turn it, resting it in one hand and turning it with the other, walking backward at the same time. Anne is frowning with concentration, her forehead furrowed. After a few turns she looks up at him in delight. There, attached to her hook, is a short length of perfectly twisted rope of hay, coming out from the haycock itself and growing as she turns the handle. Joe smiles at her and calls John over. He shows John how to guide the hay out of the haycock, easing it so that it always comes out in an even thickness.

"The secret in it is this," he is saying. "Try not to let it break. You have to work together, mind, and each keep an eye out for the other. And Anne, if you see the hay begin to come out too thinly, then you must wait until John has it sorted out. And John, mind you feel the pull as she draws it out and keep your end up accordingly. And if it does break, it's matterless. Just call me and I'll set it to rights for ye."

I turn and walk back to Orla, and all the rest of the afternoon I keep an eye out for Anne, waiting for her to give up and throw down her tool. John gives up on his end after an hour or two, so that Carmel takes over. But Anne never pauses. And whenever she has to stop, to watch the two ropes that she's made being flung over the haycocks and tugged hard into place at the bases with the wooden pegs, she looks so proud.

"Sure Jaysus, Mary, hasn't your sister got great patience!" I start and turn at Nuala's voice. She's smiling at me and digging me in the ribs. "I can't see you keeping up a thing like that all afternoon, can you?" I flush and push her hand away. I'm jealous, I realize. Jealous of Anne, who has earned Nuala's praise. I stare at her, my sister, and see her small face light up as Billy, flinging a rope up into the sky over the hay, shouts at Daddy, "She's no waster, this one, Liam! You have a champion rope maker for a daughter."

Daddy laughs and looks at her fondly, and tears prick my eyes. I've often been jealous of her, though I hate to admit it. Jealous of her for her good looks, and for the way she's Daddy's favorite. But—and this is a shock to me—I've never had to be jealous of anything she's actually done before. I'm better at everything than she is: schoolwork, drawing, even games—though that isn't saying much. I've always pushed her away from me whenever she's come bothering me about my work. I've never let her near me! Is *that* why she's always on the lookout for me, to tell tales and so on?

I feel very strange now, leaning on my fork, looking at things this way, from another point of view. From my sister's point of view. A whole flock of little thoughts come winging into my mind; memories of incidents from the past that I've had with Anne. And as they circle around inside my head, their shapes alter, so that they look quite different, as though the light is playing on them from another angle. And now Anne has beaten me! She's done something better than I've done. Nuala and Orla have moved away from me. Are they looking at me strangely, or is it another trick of the light?

I drop my fork and walk over to Anne. She shrugs her

head away from me when she sees me coming. She's rejecting me, in case I'm about to reject her! I see that now. So I swallow my pride and walk right up to her. "You're really good at that, Anne, aren't you?" She looks up at me, and her face is wary. In another light, I might say it was spiteful. But now that I know different, I carry on. "No, really, I couldn't do that half as well as you." Her eyes dart over my face. I'm looking at her rosy face, and her hair all matted with hay, and at her grubby hands and scratched arms. She looks so sweet that I want to cuddle her.

But now I see how hard it is for me to touch someone. More precisely, to touch my sister. I have to swallow miles of pride and fear between us if I'm just to reach out and touch her. But I remember Mammy's hand, dry and warm, holding mine as we ran together over the field. And Nuala's, wiping the tears from my face and drifting over the skin of my neck.

So I put my arm around Anne's shoulders—they feel so little and slender—and I say, with my voice a little trembly, "Anne, will you make a posy for me, when you've finished that?" And now she's smiling, but trying not to show it, as she says, "I might do, if I've got time."

And I'm so pleased when, later on, she does.

✒ Forty

When the hay is all gathered and sculpted into hay-cocks, the meadows are studded with rows of little golden clumps, each one held firmly and neatly in place with its pegged-down hay ropes. And only when every-one's hay is cut and gathered in this way do we begin the business of harnessing the horses to the hay carts, to bring the hay in from the field to the hay barns. The sun is still shining, strong and clear, kind weather for the saving of the hay. And we are all turning brown from being outdoors from dawn to dusk. The spots on my face have all dried up, and the painful lumpy ones I had on my shoulders seem to have disappeared.

But even so, there is an ache in my heart. I've always loved the business of bringing in the hay. I always used to work with Dadda, on his hay cart. But this year, I'm wondering who I'll be working with. It is the very last time that the hay will be brought in in this way, and my eyes fill with tears at the thought that perhaps Billy, or even Joe, won't let me join in.

I decide to just assume that they will, and when the men set off to bring in the other horses from the far meadow I run off and bring the chestnut mare in from the field. She whickers reassurance at her foal as we leave him behind, her ears pricked up in eagerness at the thought of meeting her friends, the other horses. I lead her to the stable and fetch out the harness: the blinkers, the collar with its wooden haims, the straddle and the big loose straps of the breeches.

It gives me a great feeling of peace to be harnessing a horse for work. And even though it's a year since I've done it, my fingers know exactly what to do with each buckle and hook. With the breeches hanging loosely over her haunches, I lead the mare to the cart house to back her into the shafts of a hay cart. There is still no one about yet, back from the fields, and I work steadily, enjoying the details of tackling the mare into the shafts of the cart. I keep at bay the thought that it might be for the very last time.

I pull the long chains from the back of the shafts up over the length of her body to link them into the hooks on the haims around her neck. This is so that she is kept centered in the shafts. Then I bend down under her to catch hold of the bellyband and bring it through, from one shaft, to attach it to the shaft nearest me. This is to stop the two shafts from leaping up when the weight of the hay is loaded into the cart.

I'm just groping for the band when I see Mammy's legs walking toward us. I grab the band and pull it through, leaning my head and shoulder against the mare's warm sides to hide from Mammy. But I see her legs, brown as a berry, walk round by the mare's head, and so down toward me. I stand up, flushing, as she draws near me, tension pulling at my stomach. If she has come to stop me doing this, I won't know what to do. I can't bear it. I close my eyes.

But I hear her voice then saying, "You and I will take the mare then, shall we, Mary?" I open my eyes in time to see her awkwardly reaching for the long rope reins, which are hanging where I've looped them, around the fork of the haims. Mammy is keeping well back from the mare, her eyes glued to the flickering ears, and she jumps slightly as the mare shifts her legs and the metal shoes scrape on the concrete.

"Do you want me to do that?" I ask her hesitantly, holding out my hand to take the reins. She smiles, and my heart is thumping in my chest. I am so surprised at her. "Well, yes, allanah. Maybe I'd be better off riding on the cart." So Mammy hops onto the flat, smooth platform of the cart, dangling her legs over the side and swinging them. She looks at me as I loop the long reins over the haims again and take the mare by the ropes just below her mouth to lead her out of the gate. "It's easier if you just do this," I say, "just lead her by the bridle, really." "Is that so?" says Mammy dreamily.

As we walk slowly down the lane, me keeping an eye out for ruts so as not to jolt Mammy, I am quite amazed. This is indeed a turn up for the books! My back is tingling between my shoulder blades as I imagine Mammy's critical eyes on me from behind. And then

I hear her voice, so quiet and gentle that it doesn't even sound like hers, saying, "Ah well, sure. This is the last time that this job will be done by the horses." I turn round and see that she's looking around her over the hedgerows. "Progress and improvements," she's musing. "Ah well, sure, things would be better if they were easier. But sure, poor Dadda kept on with the horses. And now he's gone . . ."

Her voice breaks off. Her face is turned away from me, but I know that her eyes are full. I turn the mare in at the gateway of the first hayfield, the one that was the first to be cut and stacked. Mammy must approve, because she's not saying anything. I walk the mare carefully over the meadow, threading our way between the haycocks, until I reach the far corner, and then I bring her to a halt and edge her round, so that the back of the cart is facing inward to a haycock.

I pause as Mammy gets down slowly from her seat. "Damn!" I suddenly remember. "I've forgotten the ropes!" "Don't worry yourself," says Mammy. "I have them here." And as she jumps down, she puts her hands to her waist and I see that she has the thick ropes looped around her, like a belt. I smile at her. These ropes are essential for lashing the tall haycock to the cart when once we get it on there, so that it doesn't slip off on the jolting ride back to the barn.

Mammy comes up to where I'm standing by the horse's head. "Will you back her up, or will I?" she asks. My mind rapidly flicks through a few thoughts. Like she's *ask-*

ing me, not telling me. Like, she's afraid of horses still; I saw the way she handed me the reins, edging away from the mare. Like, she's taking it for granted that I know what to do. But I swallow, for I'm not sure that I do. I've always had Dadda with me before.

"I will," I say, more decisively than I feel, and so she goes back to the big lever on the cart, where the shafts join the platform. This lever is attached to a massive cog, and as she turns it, a metal tongue clatters along the teeth of the cog, and the cart is gradually lowered on the axis above its wheels. And gradually it slopes down, so that the foot-wide band of gleaming brass at its other end is resting on the ground, at the base of the haycock. Mammy casts a critical eye on it and then calls to me, "It's ready now. You're all right. Back her up."

With my head under the mare's chin, I grasp the bridle on each side of her face and urge her backward. "Go up, now, up, up," I say, as I've heard Dadda do so many times. She jerks her head up, and for one awful moment I think she's going to dig her heels in, but no, she is backing up, tensing her shoulders and gathering her haunches in under her tail. "Grand! Grand!" calls Mammy. "Keep her going the way you're doing now." The mare strains as the cart pushes right under the cock of hay, the brass edge of it sliding clean so that the hay is gradually pushed up onto the cart.

"Steady now, steady!" shouts Mammy. We have to be careful not to push back too far or the haycock will overbalance and topple over backward, which would be a disaster. But we've caught it at just the right point, and Mammy starts turning the lever again, backward, forward, then backward again. And slowly but surely, the platform of the cart is raised from its sloping position and is horizontal again, this time with the hay on top of it.

"Well, we didn't do too badly," Mammy says with a smile, as she lashes two of the ropes she's brought to the hooks at the edge of the cart. Then she jumps, with her arms straight up, tossing a rope as high as she can into the sky, to go over the top of the haycock. The rope wriggles and snakes against the blue sky, hovering directly above the hay, but then it makes up its mind and dives down, over the hay, to fall upon the shafts by the mare's tail. Mammy laughs. "I always was a good thrower," she says. "it's one of the few jobs I *could* do, when we were children." She screws up her face ruefully as she grabs the loose rope and loops it firmly inside the ring on the shaft, yanking it tightly so that it's taut over the hay and wrenching it into a good, firm knot. "That, and tying knots." She sighs.

"Well, *I'm* glad you can tie knots!" I say. "I can't do them to save my life." "Maybe we're a good team, then, Mary. What would you say?" But I blush, and cannot reply. Mammy turns from me and looks out over the meadow, her hands on her hips. "I was near killed, having to leave all this behind, when I first went over the water to England," she says. She turns to me and adds, "Give me a leg up, Mary. I want to ride back on top of the hay." I wonder, Did she used to do that with Dadda when she was little, just like I did as recently as last year?

Giggling and scrabbling, I lean myself into the hay and give her my shoulder to stand on. She gives a light spring and is up, clinging to the ropes as she scrambles upward, and then placing herself firmly astride the rounded cap at the top. I unloop the reins from around the haims and hop up between the shafts, bracing myself back against the hay as I tell the mare to guide us home by flicking at the reins.

Mammy is gazing around her, rocking dreamily above the hedgerows as we slowly walk back across the field. "Sure, I knew all these fields as well as you know your own bedroom, Mary. Almost as far as my eye can see, this land had been worked by your grandfather or Mammy's brothers, and now by Billy and Joe and Pat-Joe. And sure, you'd know anyone in the lanes passing by. And these big skies rolling past, and the sweet air. Jaysus, I was killed leaving it all, the first time I had to go away, to the grim, dark streets of Manchester."

My head rolling back in the hay, I ask her, "But why did you have to go, Mammy? If you loved it so much, couldn't Dadda have let you stay?" She gives a short bark of a laugh. "That's a fine one, that is!" she says. And as we walk back to the hay barn, to where Billy and Joe are waiting to pile the hay up to the rafters, she starts to talk to me about herself for the very first time.

✑ Forty-one

"You ask me, Mary, why did I have to go from here if I loved it so much? And why couldn't Dadda have let me stay? But sure, Dadda himself had no say in the matter, and if Dadda didn't, what choice was there in it for me?

"When I was a little child, my mammy, your granny, used to talk away to me while we worked together in the kitchen. There'd be three or four of the little ones crawling and toddling around the floor, and because I was the biggest girl she'd address her remarks to me, though I never used to understand the half of what she'd be saying. That came later, when I was older.

" 'Bridie, allanah, the heart in me is sore,' she'd say. She sometimes used to frighten me, rocking back and forth as if she was in pain. She'd grab one of the little ones onto her lap, shaking him up and down while she keened to herself. Holding him out in front of her, she'd cry, 'Have I brought ye into the world that ye should have to fly from your land, that ye should go away across the water to the four corners of the world and never see your home again?'

"Sometimes Dadda would come in and catch her at it, and he'd be angry and say to her, 'At least we have a roof over our heads! At least the land we are working is our own! At least we can keep the food that we grow!'

"But my mammy would get even angrier then. She'd put the little one down and she'd start walking around the kitchen, slamming the pots down on the table and beating her hand against the walls. 'What's the good of having our land back if we can't keep our children on it?' she'd say.

"And Dadda would look tired then, and shake his head. 'Sure, God's truth, allanah,' he'd say, 'isn't it all we can do to keep food in our bellies, without dreaming of impossibilities.' And then Mammy would grab him by the arm and drag him to the window to look out at Mount Leinster, and she'd say, 'No matter how hungry we are, we can still raise up our heads to that mountain beyond!'

"Then she'd snatch one of us up again into her arms and shake us under Dadda's nose. 'Here you are, Michael Kelly,' she'd say, her voice low and fierce, 'here is Ireland's future! And what are you going to do with it, this fine, healthy future? Throw it away, pitch it out across the water! Send it off to work for the English, cheap labor, just like we've always been! Oh, Michael, allanah, was it for this that we fought, when we struggled for Ireland's future? Was it for this that those before us died?'

"Like I've said, Mary, I didn't understand one half of the things she used to say, until I was much older. But what I did understand was that there was no money at home to support me and I grown, though I didn't know why. I only knew that one day I'd have to leave, and as I grew into my teens, I used to cry at the thought of leaving, especially during the evenings when Dadda had us all playing the fiddles and the tin whistles, and when I'd be put to dancing a jig with one of my cousins or a neighbor. They were lovely evenings, with the little ones all falling asleep like kittens on the settle in front of the fire, until someone remembered to put them in their beds.

"I used to look at these fields, at the little lanes round about me, and my heart was raw with grieving that one day I'd have to leave. I applied for a place to train as a nurse in Manchester, and I nearly died when I was accepted! Poor Dadda was so proud of me. 'There's nothing in Ireland for you, Bridie,' he used to say. 'If you go over the water to England, you'll have your own livelihood, so you will.' But that last evening, as he stood and watched me pack my bag in the yellow lamplight, I was numb with sorrow.

"So I did what we Irish have always had to do. I left my home and everything I knew, and I went all on me own across the water, to find work where the streets are paved with gold. And there were no green fields around me when I walked along those dark pavements. Didn't I have to wear a scarf over me mouth, to stop myself from choking on the thick yellow air. Oh, how I longed for the sweet air of home!

"And the buildings! God, they towered over me, like massive ships. They seemed to be plowing their way through the people on the pavements. So many people! I'd never seen so many people before in my life, nor known so few! Rushing through the streets, looking neither to the right nor to the left. Where do they all be rushing to? I used to wonder.

"The hospital was huge, with turrets like a castle in a picture book. It took me ages to get used to it. The other nurses thought I was cracked, so I found it hard to make friends. They thought I was stupid because I didn't know how to turn on an electric light until I was shown. They used to make jokes about how stupid the Irish are, and I used to pretend to laugh. But all the while how I grieved for home! I used to sing that song about the forty shades of green quietly to myself at night in bed. I slept in a long, dark room with twenty others, and God help me, didn't the tears sometimes roll down my cheeks and into my mouth, while I tried not to make a sound.

"I thought I'd die of loneliness sometimes, Mary. But somehow the work kept me going. I could forget myself when I was working with the patients, and sure they, poor souls, were glad enough to talk to me in their hour of need. I nursed men whose lungs were burned by poisonous fumes, women who'd worked all their lives caring for the rich people and who now had only me to care for them, little children whose bodies hadn't grown properly, all swollen from hunger, with their skins all raw and septic from lice and so on. God help them, I'd never seen such suffering before.

"Many a time I used to wonder how it was, that if the English had so much in the way of wealth—for hadn't they had our land as well as their own, for centuries—how was it that there was still so much suffering and hunger, among English people, in an English hospital.

"But most of the time, I longed to go home. Not a night went by that I didn't ache with longing to go home as I lay in my little iron bed. But at home they were in such need of the money I sent, with all the little ones to feed and no market for our cattle. I used to save every penny I earned, either to send it home to Dadda or to put toward my passage home. I didn't even dare dream of my holidays, when I'd be able to go home, because it used to hurt me too much.

"And then one day I had a letter from Dadda, asking me to send him £15. He wanted it to put it toward the purchase of a new horse. He said in his letter, 'If I can buy this horse, then your brother Billy will be able to go out to work as a hired plowman and earn the money for the keep of the little ones.' Jaysus, I was in agony! Tears poured down onto the envelope as I sealed it up, with all the money I'd saved up to go home inside it. It took me two years, two long and lonely years, before I could save it all up again. Two years of loneliness in England, while my heart ached to be home.

"I remember it was then that I started going to the

church, any odd time I had. I used to go and kneel in front of the statue of Our Lady, and light a candle for Mammy and Dadda and all the little ones. I used to say my prayers, a whole rosary every time I was there, to still the grieving murmurs of my heart. I hated it in England, Mary, and I used to pray for forgiveness. And the peace and quiet in the church used to calm me down. On Sundays, at Mass, the priests were all Irish, and the sound of their voices used to make me feel almost as though I was home.

"Many a time I used to have a laugh to myself at how peculiar it was, that I'd had to sell my fare home for a horse! I had to work hard to stop myself from hating the beast, for I'd never even seen him! I had to remind myself of how much Dadda loved horses, and how important they were in the work of the land and in growing food so that the little ones wouldn't starve.

"And now here we are, bringing in the hay with the help of a horse for the very last time! I should be glad, sure! Tractors will help the farmers, and that can be no bad thing. And isn't it grand that Billy has managed to save the money to buy one! But it's sadness I'm feeling, to my great surprise.

"I wonder what Dadda would think of it all, if he knew? He's only just left us, and things are changing so fast. I'll remember this day, and how the fields are looking now, forever. Doesn't it make you wonder, Mary, to think that when we go back to London, if we go up

high to look at the view we'll see nothing but buildings
and roads as far as the eyes on us can reach? And the
fields and the forests and mountain will be nothing but
a dream."

🦢 Forty-two

Nuala has kept her word, and I am finding a friend in my mammy. My heart is so light that even the prospect of Mass today doesn't bother me. Yes, it's Sunday—but Sunday with a difference. It's the first Sunday after the hay harvest: everyone's hay is in, and the weather hasn't stopped smiling on us. Everyone is in holiday spirits; I actually heard Joe's voice hooting with laughter over something that Nuala was saying to him in the cow shed earlier. And now he's out with Daddy in the lane, the two of them yelling at each other as they take it in turns to drive the tractor up to the meadow gateway and back again. The tricky bit in the middle, where they have to turn the tractor round without getting the wheels jammed in the ditch, actually has Joe shouting at Daddy, between his gales of laughter.

Daddy's face is rosy, but he avoids my eyes. Something has changed between him and me since the night he hit me. He doesn't talk to me much, and when he does, his voice is quiet.

But Mammy, now! Things are different there! We're getting dressed for Mass, and, slightly nervously, I'm putting on my yellow minidress. She isn't even batting an eyelid. My legs are nice and brown, not as dark as hers, but not red and sunburned either. So I don't bother with stockings. And John is in a short-sleeved aertex shirt, with no tie!

As we walk up the pathway to the church, I notice how well everyone is looking, all tanned and relaxed looking, chatting easily. We're all looking forward to what is going to happen after Mass. There's going to be a dinner and dance in Donnelly's, next to the church, to celebrate the hay. Nuala's looking lovely, in a short white skirt, and people are looking at us as we walk up the path. I hope they're not critical of the length of our skirts, but walking next to Nuala, I don't care!

Mass goes on as usual, with me sitting up in the gallery with the women. The sermon isn't too long, because the priest knows that no one's mind will be on it, what with the dance coming up afterward. He just says a short prayer for the good weather to continue for the ripening and harvesting of the corn and that is it, really.

After the final blessing and "Go in Peace," all the men get up and begin to file out over the wooden boards, but none of the women is stirring. It is only when all the men have left the church that we begin to move. As I slowly follow after the women funneling down the stairs, I gaze out over the main body of the church and see that instead of going out the door, the women are all slowly moving up the aisle, toward the altar.

"Nuala!" I whisper. "What are we doing?" "Going to light a candle to the Holy Mother," she murmurs back.

Slowly, we make our way up the nave. It feels strange to me to be among a large crowd that is composed solely of women. It's like participating in a secret, from which the men have been excluded. Except I don't know what the secret is either.

At the foot of the altar I can see the two statues, flanked by heaps of flowers and blossoms. All the women are congregating round them. One is a statue that I know well, Mary, Our Lady; the other is of a woman dressed in green, with a red petticoat showing under her long robe. She is gazing out at us, resting one hand on the pommel of a large sword which is leaning against her thigh and stretching out her other hand toward us, a bunch of herbs held in its fingers. Around her feet there are growing small white flowers, and shamrocks are peeping out from between her toes.

"Nuala," I whisper again. "Who's that supposed to be?" "That's Saint Brigit, one of the patron saints of Ireland," says Nuala. "Your mammy is named after her."

Mammy has been coming along behind us, arm in arm with Granny, and she nudges me in the back and gives me two pennies. She leans forward to do the same to Anne, who is a little ahead of us. "Light a candle, both of you," she hisses.

We wait our turn. Already so many candles have been lit to them that the statues seem to be floating on pyramids of flame. And so many women are praying that the church is filled with waves of liquid sound. It's a sound I've never heard before, completely different from the sound of the congregation praying when all the men are present. The women are using their voices as though the sounds they make are more important than the words they use. There is a sighing, keening sound, whose pitch sends shivers down my back. The flames and the voices are trembling in the air and swelling up, as though breaking through time and space.

I blink and squeeze my eyes together to stop myself feeling dizzy, and keep myself focused on all the faces around me instead. Small clasped hands, rough with millions of washdays, are joined under faces all weathered with the wind and the rain. They have worked so hard, all their lives, these women, and now they are gazing at these statues, praying for their families, for their children far away in other lands, for the crops and for the animals. None of them seems to be praying for herself. Such complete devotion makes me angry. But it awes me too.

I follow their gaze to the statues. Mary, the Blessed Virgin, is looking down at us like some figure from Nuala's book. Her face is huge and broad, like the full moon, and her elongated eyes and wide mouth are smiling. And this smile is like the smile that's in your heart when you run through the grasses on a sunny day. It's so serene, so all-seeing and all-knowing, that it contains the reason why the trees grow and the birds sing. I am lost in that smile as I gaze at it.

The women's voices are soaring and swooping and I am lifted up by them. The statue of Brigit is smiling too, and her sword is glittering with flame. The voices flow around the candles and the flowers. They are conjuring a spell of sound out of the air.

I put my two pennies in the metal container and hold a candle to a burning flame. The dark wick droops and then drops off, burning, leaving behind a small white spear of flame. I press it into the molten wax at the base of the candleholder, and the flame yearns and stretches, upright and swaying. I am swimming upward with it, this bright darting arrow of light.

I am fused with the steady tongue of flame. Granny's voice is rising and falling. "May he rest in peace, oh, great white mother Mary, oh, Brid the lovely fair." The sound of the voices is filling me. My skin is tingling with it, and my head has melted into it.

When we leave the church, my head is still soaring. Somehow, we have summoned up all that is brightest, all that is best, among the candle flames and the flowers. And this swirling, glowing sound is flowing outward from the church, up into the sky, and chasing the dark mists of fear away. The bright blade of Brigit's sword is flashing.

I bless myself in the big scallop shell in the doorway, without having to be nagged into it by Mammy. The cool drops splashing my face seem quite appropriate to-day, part of the flames, and the flowers, and the magic sounds.

Forty-three

And now, all that we have to do is eat a huge meal and then dance through the long afternoon. Many people have been fasting for hours because they've been to Holy Communion, so the long tables filled with food at Donnelly's are soon tucked into.

Donnelly's place is the only shop in the village. It's the post office and the general store, and it has a bar as well, so that people can settle themselves after the tiresome business of filling out forms or buying nails. Or ordering coffins, for Mr. Donnelly is also the undertaker. Which makes sense, really, him being so near the church.

His place was built by the English; he took it over when they left. It used to be the lodge of the Big House, which is now burned out and crow filled a mile across the fields. There are two huge rooms at the back, behind the bar and store, and they open onto Donnelly's home meadow, where he grazes a few sheep. It is in these interconnecting rooms that the food is laid out for us.

Eggs and ham and bread and salad and potatoes are

piled on top of vast oak tables, whose legs are carved with odd-looking monsters and swathed in garlands of imaginary vegetation. These tables are left over from the English days, as are the massive oak and leather settles and chairs ranged round them. The leather on the chairs is so old and shiny that it looks and feels like wood. All this furniture must be hundreds of years old. The backs of the chairs and settles tower behind us as we sit on them.

The fiddler is playing on his own as we eat, a pleasant sound in the background. We're all full of the sense of it being a most unusual thing to do, to sit and eat, all of us together, on a Sunday, with music and dance to follow. Everyone is here: the babies and the children, and the very old people, and the two crippled men who talk to themselves and wander shakily around the tables. "God bless the mark," says everyone as they pass by, and we hand them food and drink, which they sometimes eat and sometimes don't.

As more and more people leave the table to gather with their glasses on the grass in the meadow the band settles down to play, and in no time we are all lepping and whooping to the wild and joyful music. I bump into Orla and we do a jig together, straightbacked, keeping our arms hanging motionless by our sides while our legs fly like ribbons into the air. Orla's footwork is dead fancy; mine is simpler, but just as gay.

I run back, laughing, to where Mammy is standing.

She's saying something to a couple of the older women who are sitting on chairs next to her. "Ah sure, it's not too short, Nana. In England now, they do be wearing them a lot shorter. And indeed, isn't the color lovely on her." As I get my breath back, I could kiss Mammy. Imagine her sticking up for me like that!

I link my arm in hers, and we watch together as the men all set off on a Kerry reel. To my surprise, they all stand back while my daddy shows off some of the most cunning and wicked bits of stepping. They are all whooping and cheering him to encourage him on his way, and he flies and whirls and stamps and spins for ages. Then Pat-Joe hops in and draws him back, and all the men do a little step back and forth in front of him in turn. They are telling him that he's cock of the yard. Then they all stand separate again and do the click dance, stamping their hard shoes so forcefully on the ground that the grass is entirely pulverized.

The musicians are shouting and yelling at each other in Irish, the fiddler's arm pumping like a piston, and the hand of the drummer is whisking his stick so fast against the skin of the bodhran that you can only see a blur. Then, with one last roar, they bring it to a standstill, and the men stop dancing, laughing their heads off. They are all breathless and red faced, slapping each other on the back and telling Daddy that England hasn't dried him up entirely. I walk over to him and say, "That was brilliant, Daddy! I didn't know you could do that!" He twinkles at one of the men and says, "Aye, well, there's many a thing you don't know about me yet, so there is." And his eyes hold mine for a second.

The musicians are resting, sending out little plucks or twangs into the air as they settle their instruments. Then the man with the tin whistle stamps his foot for silence and holds out his arm. He is asking us all to look at Orla, who is sitting on one of Donnelly's bar stools, her knees tucked up and her feet tucked in. Her back is straight and her hands are folded in her lap. When everyone is quiet, she begins to sing, all alone, with no accompaniment at all.

It is in Irish, her song, and I can't understand the words, but I know what it is saying. It tears at my heart and fills my eyes with tears. Her voice plunges low, into the long, deep swells of sorrow and sadness, drawing out the vowel sounds like the long, deep sigh of the wind in the rafters of an empty house.

And now it is soaring up into the air, into the flight of the lark in the morning, darting and twisting and propelling itself up, up into the sky, with hope and longing so intense that it sends shivers down my spine. Then it trills into the running water, and dances over the stones, and laughs at you and teases you, so that you can't help laughing out loud, its cheeky fingers tweaking your ears and pulling at your hair.

Then a pause, and then the long swells again, and then the lark drawing you out into the trees, into the highest branches, and then, just as it has you poised in the pure, blue sky, it halts, quite suddenly, and leaves you there. There is silence for a moment, and then Orla smiles and bows her head, and we all roar and cheer and clap at her for what she has given us.

Orla gets down off her stool and laughs as people praise her, and then all the little boys and girls come out, dressed in their white shirts and gold sashes and embroidered shawls, looking so proud that they are almost bursting with seriousness. Their little feet in the black pumps flitter over the grass, whisking among the daisies and the buttercups. They weave so nicely in and out of their two lines, their small shoulders straight and their backs held stiff. Granny and all the older people are smiling and clapping, sitting on the tall chairs to one side, merry and rosy over their port wine and their sherry.

Mammy gives me a glass of sherry mixed with lemonade. She says, "Don't have too much now, in this heat, or the head on you will split open and burst." I can quite believe it; just one glass makes me feel all spinny. "Isn't this great, Mammy?" I say. "There's nothing like this in England, is there, everyone of all ages and sizes going somewhere to have fun like this, dancing and drinking stout and sherry, and getting drunk on the music?"

Mammy sighs and says, "No, there isn't, more's the pity. So just you enjoy it while you can!" Orla comes up and says how nice my dress is, so I say she can have it. I can always make another one when I get home. She's delighted but a bit worried in case her daddy won't let her wear it. But then Pat-Joe comes up and puts his arm around me and says how well it looks—so that's him sorted out!

The last dance of the afternoon, before everyone has to get home for the milking and so on, is the most amazing. And it seems to last for hours. People are milling about in the meadow, some dancing, some coming and going, when suddenly something happens to the musicians. They seem to take off, to leap over the horizon bounding time and space, a bit like the women's voices in the church. They are playing a reel, and the deep and heavy beat of the bodhran is sending shivers down my spine. It is making my feet move so fast that I have no control over them. It is the drum that is pulling them into motion, the deep pulse of passion, like blood throbbing in the earth beneath my feet. Instead of me dancing to the music, the music seems to be dancing me. My blood and my bones, my muscles and my brain, are all completely absorbed by the wild and skirling sounds, and I have lost myself completely.

Then the fiddles and whistles are whirling and swooping, and everyone is dancing, linking arms in the reel and dancing together before skipping on to do the same with the next person. It is as though we are all being woven by the music into a vast ribbon of movement and laughter. I grab the arm nearest me and see that it is Anne's face that's laughing into mine. We whirl each other round and round and round until our momentum flings us away from each other to grab someone else and begin the same mad twirling again. I dance with everyone, with Mammy and Daddy, with all my cousins, with Pat-Joe and Billy, with Joe and with Nuala. Lovely Nuala, whose bright flushed face is beaming at mine as it slowly dawns on me what I will say to her soon.

Right to the very edges of the meadow, wildly dancing people are weaving in long lines, plaiting together and braiding like the grasses in the wind. We are spread out in ripples, like a vast watermark on the grass. And then the music pulls the ripples wider and slows them down until we all come to a halt with the last stretch of the fiddler's arm. We all say our good-byes and walk home, arm in arm, to the animals.

Forty-four

A long, low, terrible pain is in my heart. When I eat my dinner, the sweet taste of Granny's butter melting into the potatoes brings tears to my eyes. With my head bowed, my hair hides my face, and I struggle to swallow my mouthful of food while my throat constricts with tears.

This is the last time I'll have dinner here for ages. Granny sits on the hearth, rocking back and forth, and everyone is silent, except for Billy, who's making jokes that no one laughs at, not even John. Daddy can't wait to leave the table, and Billy and Joe follow him out, grabbing bottles of stout from the table to finish in the warm evening outside.

We all sit round the table, awkward and silent. I'm grateful to Nuala when she gets up from her seat and starts bossing us around. "Anne! John! Pick up these plates and help your mammy with the washing up, will ye!" Grumbling, "Oh, Nuala, why?" "We never do the washing up!" they stand unwillingly round the table. "All the more reason to start now!" she snaps, and grabs my arm. "Come up with me, Mary, and gather those clothes from the fire. We'll take them upstairs and start the packing."

Mammy raises her head. "No . . . Nuala . . . I'll do it in a minute." "Bridie, you will not," she says. Our last night here, and still Mammy hasn't started our packing! She had the suitcases packed for a week before we left England.

Numbly, I gather up the clothes that have been airing round the hearth. I bury my face in them as I bundle them up, breathing in the sweet scents of the air of Ireland, of the leaves in the haggard. And I gulp as tears fill my eyes again.

"Mammy," Nuala is talking to Granny. "Did you pack the parcel?" Granny starts, and slowly raises herself to her feet. "Sure God, I did not!" she says, and is instantly a-bustle. "Nuala, fetch me the box, that little brown box I was saving. Bridie, will you go and pick yourself a bit of butter from the back kitchen. I haven't even cut the rashers yet, and I was almost forgetting the cake!" Granny is herself again, organizing the parcel of food that she always makes for Mammy to take back to England with her. The parcel that is full of the tastes of home.

Everyone is busy again now, moving around the kitchen. Mammy is scolding John and Anne as they unwillingly start to pile up the plates and dishes. "No! Not the white-handled knives! Sure, honest to God, what

have you between your two ears at all? Put them into
this jug, the way the hot water won't scald the handles.
They're your granny's best bone-handled knives!"

Nuala pushes me across the kitchen out of the door.
"What's the matter with you, Mary? Have you dozed
off on your feet?" But the touch of her hand lingers
gently between my shoulder blades.

Upstairs, I drop the clothes onto the bed, and Nuala
starts busily sorting and smoothing and folding. "Here,
you take the skirts and shorts, and I'll do the shirts and
blouses." The realization that we really do have to leave
all this, that it's all going to end tomorrow, makes me
feel almost stunned. It's only Nuala's darting eyes and
busy hands that get me going.

I feel all thumbs at first, trying to fold the clothes, but
slowly the rhythm of doing the work comes back to me,
and in a little while I'm almost soothed as I fold the
crisp, dry garments. It's a relief, having something to do
to keep my mind off the awful sadness.

Nuala's voice is so cheerful, I can hardly believe it.
She's chattering on about a job she might go for in Carlow, and about the temperature in her friend's room in
New York at this time of year. I let her words wash over
me, not really listening. But then I realize she's stopped
suddenly, and through my numbness I see that she's
looking at me expectantly.

"Well, did you?" she's saying.

"Sorry, Nuala, did I what?" I stammer.

"Did you come up with your side of the bargain?"

What on earth is she talking about? I struggle to travel back into my mind, to remember what I'm supposed to have done. Then, "Oh! . . . Yes!" I say, and I sink down onto the bed. Of course, she's asking me for advice about those imaginary children of hers in New York.

I fiddle with John's shorts in my lap. Was it only a couple of days ago, in the wild field of dancing people, that I felt so sure of myself? That I thought I knew what I'd say to Nuala if she asked me again? Voices ripple up from the yard outside, where Daddy and my uncles are sitting by the wall in the evening sun. Our last night! But Nuala's voice won't let me sink back into sadness. "Well, don't keep me in suspense, for the love of God! What advice have you for me?" Hands on hips, she can't be ignored.

I raise my head and gaze at the wall. For a moment I'm back, walking along the track on my colt, in the land of Niamh, near Maeve's rath in the drowsy, humming lanes. I'm back in the kitchen, listening to Granny, back with Dadda checking the straps of the trap, back in the merry haymaking, in the wild dancing afterward . . . Oh, yes . . .

I look at Nuala, and my voice is so full that it comes out in a whisper, "I'd . . . I'd tell them about . . . all this," I say, trying to open my hands out and show her it all. "I'd tell them everything . . . everything about this place that I could remember . . ." My hands drop back into my lap and I fall silent, afraid I'm going to cry, hiding my face in my hair again. I don't want to cry, not now. I raise my head up again and look at her as I say, "It's something to be proud of, isn't it, Nuala?"

Quietly she's saying, "It is that, allanah, it is that." And I lean against her shoulder for a minute when she sits down beside me. I feel my jawline hardening as I clench my two rows of teeth together, and I draw away from her and sit up straight, facing her.

"It's nothing to be ashamed of, coming from here. And if your friends laugh at you ... your kids' friends, I mean ... if they laugh at you for being, you know, Irish ... it doesn't mean there's anything wrong with you, does it?" She's smiling at me, and I wonder why her eyes are filled with tears. But I'm not crying, though my voice is trembling as I continue. "It means there's something wrong with *them*, really, doesn't it? It means that they don't know any better, sort of. So you'd have to tell them, wouldn't you, how lovely it is here, and how ... how sad it is to have to leave ... and why it was you had to go. And you'd have to hope they'd understand, in the end. But if they didn't ... well, some of them might ... But if they didn't, it wouldn't be anything wrong with you ..."

"And you'd have to be strong, and not get upset," Nuala is saying quietly. "As strong as that Queen Maeve, I'm thinking ..."

The door of the bedroom is opening. Slowly we turn and look, and there is Mammy, her face crumpling and quivering, her hands held out stiffly in front of her. She puts them to her face and buries her head in them, her body frozen rigid, not making a sound. I start up, terrified. I've never even seen my mammy like this before. But Nuala is there before me, leading her to the bed, sitting her down, cradling her in her arms.

And only now do Mammy's tears start to fall, in hacking sobs that it hurts me to hear. I want to help her, but I don't know how. My hands are dangling uselessly. Nuala is stroking her face, rocking her, like she did with me that time before. Mammy's voice is broken with anguish, stricken with sorrow. "OOOoooh, Nuala . . . how in God's name . . . how am I to bear it . . . how am I to bear it at all?" . . . Nuala is giving her a hanky, crooning in her ear, soothing her as if she was a baby.

I'm panic-stricken, hearing my mother's sobs. I'm scared of what will happen now that she's broken down. And the great heaving wrenches tearing from her chest seem to be lacerating her heart. She's in such pain, and I don't know what I can do to stop it hurting her so much. Nuala knows how to help her, but all I can do is to stand here on my own, useless and in the way. And I want to do more, so much more.

She doesn't want me in here, watching her suffering, and it's frightening me to see it. I go to the door, and catch Nuala's eyes looking at me gratefully. I slip out quietly, closing the door behind me. I stand there on the landing, leaning my forehead against the cool wood. When we get back to England, who will comfort her then?

This is the first time I've ever seen her cry, but I know she must have felt sorrow before ... After Dadda died, for instance. Has she always done her crying away from us, in secret, then? Doesn't she think we could help her? Oh, Mammy! I close my eyes and squeeze them to stop my tears from falling. Will I be able to help her in England? Or am I a stranger to her, this daughter of hers who was born in a foreign land?

I think I could help her there, if she'd let me. I speak the language, after all. If I could learn how to open doors for myself, I could open doors for her. Could I do this, instead of standing lonely, with my eyes closed, behind them?

✒ Forty-five

The last morning. I do my best to help Mammy, checking under the beds and in the wardrobe, going from room to room to make sure we've left nothing behind. I help Daddy carry down the suitcases and butter the bread when Nuala's making sandwiches for us. I can't imagine wanting to eat them, though. I tell John to sit quietly with a book, so as not to spoil his clean clothes.

But just before it's time to leave, I run out into the sun and rush about the yard. "Good-bye," I whisper to the calves, to the ducks and chickens, to the cats and kittens as they scamper from my flying feet. "Oh, Prince and Molly, good-bye," I breathe into their thick and glossy coats. And I stand silently trembling in front of the charred and blackened sow-house walls. I daren't stay too long; Mammy and Daddy might be waiting, and if I hesitate, I know my tears will start to fall.

So I run from hay barn to stable, breathing in the scents of hay and straw, touching my face to the mossy stones, skimming the wood with my fingers. I want to take it all, to wrap it in my arms and take it home with me, to keep it as it is forever. There's no time for tears, not even when I bury my face into the neck of the chestnut mare and hug her close to me, not even when her muzzle gently whickers over my hair, not even when her foal trots beside me as I run back to the gate.

I don't even cry when, piled high with our suitcases, splashed with holy water, the trap jolts out of the gateway and I see Granny, standing so small and silent, with one hand waving by the kitchen door. I turn and follow the lane unfurling behind me, trying to fix on my memory the bend by the gateway wall, with Prince grinning as he turns away from us and lopes back into the yard.

At the little gray station; we all avoid each other's eyes. Our farewells are mute on the empty platform. And during the whole of the silent journey to the harbor in the north, my face is stiff and my eyes are dry. Mammy does not say a word. She gazes out of the window, and none of us speaks while Ireland is flying by.

At the port, I follow Daddy's orders silently. Heaving the luggage up the gangway. Stowing it in the cabin. Watching the little gray buildings bob up and down in the porthole. Feeling the walls of the tiny room press inward. A pain is tightening in my chest. I think I know why Mammy isn't crying.

Mumbling something, I am out the door. I stumble through narrow corridors and up lurching stairways. There is a lump in my throat I cannot swallow. I've got to be on my own.

On the top deck at last, dazzled by sunlight dancing on water. I cling to the rail. The siren blasts its dirge across the water. And slowly the thudding pistons are tugging Ireland away from me behind a screaming flock of seagulls.

The gulls are hovering and darting in front of the horizon. The mountains are getting smaller and smaller. My eyes are trying to hold them—but it's no good. Everything is racing past me while my fingers clutch in vain. The distance is growing, and soon there'll be nothing but a faint haze.

I turn away. I don't want to see it all become colorless and blurred and far away. With the sun behind me now, my shadow grows longer on the wooden deck. I gulp as I realize it's even nearer England than I am. The air is sharp with salt and it rasps the breath from my chest.

The sky is vast and blue ahead of me and white clouds wisp, like horses' tails, over the water.

☙Glossary

aertex: English brand name for fine cotton material, woven with tiny holes in it, which is used for sports shirts and casual wear.

allanah: Irish term of endearment, like "little darling"

bodhran: Irish, pronounced "borawn": an Irish drum shaped like a very large tambourine though without the metal bits. It is held in one hand by cross-struts while beaten with a double-headed stick held in the other hand, thus producing a lovely resonant, rippling, rolling sound.

bonhams: Irish, pronounced "bonavs": piglets

Bovril: English brand name: a thick, black, concentrated extract of beef, sold in black jars, used for beef tea or beef stock

brack: a rich Irish fruit bread, in which the dried fruit (sultanas, currants, and raisins) is first soaked in cold tea before being added to the mixture

breeches: here used to denote the part of the horse's harness that fits over the rump or backside of the animal. Made of leather straps, it has buckles and straps attached that are fastened onto corresponding rings in the shafts of a cart, plough, etc.

cod: Irish, nonsense or exaggeration, as in "whisht your owld cod": don't talk such nonsense

Dettol: English brand name: a disinfectant with a distinctive and pungent odor

forms: simple wooden benches with no backs

God bless the mark: Irish expression, used when in the presence of someone with any kind of disability or "mark," whether physical or mental; used also by devout people, for whom a "mark" given by God would require a prayer for God's blessing

grizzles, grizzling: the fretful crying or whimpering of a child

haggard: Irish, the area behind a house where vegetables might be grown, rubbish disposed of, laundry hung out to dry, etc.

haims: part of a horse's harness. The haims are two curved pieces of wood that are joined by a chain at one end, fitted over the padded collar around the horse's neck and attached by straps at the top, behind the horse's ears. The long reins are guided through loops at the top of this contraption so that they stay clear of the horse's legs and the shafts of the cart, passing instead along the length of the horse's back.

having a gas: Irish, having a really good time

hoardings: large billboards

howneyman: The phrase "by the howneyman" was often used in the Irish country in the same way that you would say "by God," as in, "By God, I'll beat them one day," to express a determined intention to do something.

jumper: English, a woollen sweater

knickers: underpants, usually a girl's underpants

last: a metal implement, shaped in the form of soles and heels, used by shoemakers when repairing boots and shoes

lepping: Irish, jumping up and down

mineral: In Ireland this word means fizzy drinks, like lemonade or orangade or indeed Coca-Cola

Oxo tin: Oxo cubes are cubes of dried beef stock, individually wrapped in foil. Until the 1950s they were sold in oblong tins that were enameled with the distinctive red-and-white Oxo logo. People used to recycle these tins as containers for old letters, nuts and bolts, pieces of string, or as lunch boxes for sandwiches to go into.

press: Irish word meaning "cupboard"; "hot press" means airing cupboard.

rath: a prehistoric hill fort. In Ireland many of them have come down in popular memory as being the sites of the palaces of ancient kings and queens.

reel: an Irish dance

settle: a bench with high backs and arms, often placed by a fire to keep the heat in and the drafts out. Made to fit many people, it often had a chest under the seat for storing linen.

shreel: Irish, used to denote a slovenly person, usually a woman

skirling: used to denote the whirling, soaring sound of violins and pipes and whistles

straddle: the part of a horse's harness that fits across the animal's back, like a saddle. It has a ridge in the middle, inside which is placed the chain that passes from one shaft to another of a cart or wagon.

STs: sanitary towels

tacklings: generic term for the tack of a horse; all of the harness

Tir na N'Og: The Land of Youth; "tir" means land, or country in Irish.

tube: underground train network in London; specifically, subway train

turf (peat): the form of fuel most widely used in Ireland to make a fire

underground: underground train network in London, specifically, the subterranean passages leading to platforms

whisht: Used very commonly in Ireland, it means "be quiet" or "hush" or "shut up," depending on the speaker's tone of voice.

wireless: radio

woad: a plant from which a blue dye used to be extracted. The ancient Britons used to paint themselves with woad, which terrified the Romans.